DEMIAN

THE STORY OF A YOUTH

BY HERMANN HESSE

WITH A FOREWORD BY

THOMAS MANN

Martino Publishing
Mansfield Centre, CT
2011

Martino Publishing
P.O. Box 373,
Mansfield Centre, CT 06250 USA

www.martinopublishing.com

ISBN 978-1-61427-026-3

© *2011 Martino Publishing*

Cover design by T. Matarazzo

Printed in the United States of America On 100% Acid-Free Paper

DEMIAN

THE STORY OF A YOUTH

BY HERMANN HESSE

WITH A FOREWORD BY

THOMAS MANN

HENRY HOLT AND COMPANY

FOREWORD

A FULL DECADE has passed since I last shook Hermann Hesse's hand. Indeed the time seems even longer, so much has happened meanwhile—so much has happened in the world of history and, even amid the stress and uproar of this convulsive age, so much has come from the uninterrupted industry of our own hand. The outer events, in particular the inevitable ruin of unhappy Germany, both of us foresaw and both lived to witness— far removed from each other in space, so far that at times no communication was possible, yet always together, always in each other's thoughts. Our paths in general take clearly separate courses through the land of the spirit, at a formal distance one from the other. And yet in some sense the course is the same, in some sense we are indeed fellow pilgrims and brothers, or perhaps I should say, a shade less intimately, confrères; for I like to think of our relationship in the terms of the meeting between his Joseph Knecht and the Benedictine friar Jacobus in *Glasperlenspiel* which cannot take place without the "playful and prolonged ceremony of endless bowings like the salutations between two saints or princes of the church"—a half ironic ceremonial, Chinese in character, which Knecht greatly enjoys and of which, he remarks, Magister Ludi Thomas von der Trave was also past master.

Thus it is only natural that our names should be mentioned together from time to time, and even when this happens in the strangest of ways it is agreeable to us. A well-known elderly composer in Munich, obstinately German and bitterly angry, in a recent letter to America called us both, Hesse and me, "wretches" because we do not believe that we Germans are the highest and noblest of peoples, "a canary among a flock of sparrows." The simile itself is peculiarly weak and fatuous quite apart from the ignorance, the incorrigible arrogance which it expresses and which one would think had brought misery enough to this ill-fated people. For my own part, I accept with resignation this verdict of the "German soul." Very likely in my own country I was nothing but a gray sparrow of the intellect among a flock of emotional Harz songsters, and so in 1933 they were heartily glad to be rid of me, though today they make a great show of being deeply injured because I do not return. But Hesse? What ignorance, what lack of culture, to banish this nightingale (for, true enough, he is no middle-class canary) from its German grove, this lyric poet whom Moerike would have embraced with emotion, who has produced from our language images of purest and most delicate form, who

vi

created from it songs and aphorisms of the most profound artistic insight—to call him a "wretch" who betrays his German heritage simply because he holds the idea separate from the form which so often debases it, because he tells the people from whom he sprang the truth which the most dreadful experiences still cannot make them understand, and because the misdeeds committed by this race in its self-absorption stirred his conscience.

If today, when national individualism lies dying, when no single problem can any longer be solved from a purely national point of view, when everything connected with the "fatherland" has become stifling provincialism and no spirit that does not represent the European tradition as a whole any longer merits consideration, if today the genuinely national, the specifically popular, still has any value at all—and a picturesque value may it retain—then certainly the essential thing is, as always, not vociferous opinion but actual accomplishment. In Germany especially, those who were least content with things German were always the truest Germans. And who could fail to see that the educational labors alone of Hesse the man of letters—here I am leaving the creative writer completely out of account—the devoted universality of his activities as editor and collector, have a specifically German quality? The concept of "world literature," originated by Goethe, is most natural and native to him. One of his works, which has in fact appeared in America, "published in the public interest by authority of the Alien Property Custodian, 1945," bears just this title: "Library of World Literature"; and is proof of vast and enthusiastic reading, of especial familiarity with the temples of Eastern wisdom, and of a noble humanistic intimacy with the "most ancient and holy testimonials of the human spirit." Special studies of his are the essays on Francis of Assisi and on Boccaccio dated 1904, and his three papers on Dostoevski which he called *Blick ins Chaos* (Glance into Chaos). Editions of medieval stories, of novelle and tales by old Italian writers, oriental fairy tales, *Songs of the German Poets,* new editions of Jean Paul, Novalis and other German romantics bear his name. They represent labor, veneration, selection, editing, re-issuing and the writing of informed prefaces—enough to fill the life of many an erudite man of letters. With Hesse it is mere superabundance of love (and energy!), an active hobby in addition to his personal, most extraordinarily personal, work—work which for the many levels of thought it touches and its concern with the problems of the world and the self is without peer among his contemporaries.

Moreover even as a poet he likes the rôle of editor and archivist, the game of masquerade behind the guise of one who "brings to light" other people's papers. The greatest example of this is the sublime work of his old age, *Glasperlenspiel,* drawn from all sources of human culture, both East and West, with its subtitle "Attempt at a Description of the Life of Magister Ludi Thomas Knecht, Together with Knecht's Posthumous Writings, Edited by Hermann Hesse." In reading it I very strongly felt (as I wrote to him at that time) how much the element of parody, the fiction and persiflage of a biography based upon learned conjectures, in short the verbal playfulness, help keep within limits this late work, with its dangerously advanced intellectuality, and contribute to its dramatic effectiveness.

German? Well, if that's the question, this late work together with all the earlier work is indeed German, German to an almost impossible degree, German in its blunt refusal to try to please the world, a refusal that in the end will be neutralized, whatever the old man may do, by world fame: for the simple reason that this is Germanic in the old, happy, free and intellectual sense to which the name of Germany owes its best repute, to which it owes the sympathy of mankind. This chaste and daring work, full of fantasy and at the same time highly intellectual, is full of tradition, loyalty, memory, secrecy—without being in the least derivative. It raises the intimate and familiar to a new intellectual, yes, revolutionary level—revolutionary in no direct political or social sense but rather in a psychic, poetical one: in genuine and honest fashion it is prophetic of the future, sensitive to the future. I do not know how else to describe the special, ambiguous and unique charm it holds for me. It possesses the romantic timbre, the tenuousness, the complex, hypochondriacal humor of the German soul—organically and personally bound up with elements of a very different and far less emotional nature, elements of European criticism and of psychoanalysis. The relationship of this Swabian writer of lyrics and idylls to the erotological "depth psychology" of Vienna, as for example it is expressed in *Narziss und Goldmund,* a poetic novel unique in its purity and fascination, is a spiritual paradox of the most appealing kind. It is no less remarkable and characteristic than this author's attraction to the Jewish genius of Prague, Franz Kafka, whom he early called an "uncrowned king of German prose," and to whom he paid critical tribute at every opportunity—long before Kafka's name had become so fashionable in Paris and New York.

If he is "German," there is certainly nothing plain or homely about him. The electrifying influence exercised on a whole generation just after the First World War by *Demian,* from the pen of a certain mysterious Sinclair, is unforgettable. With uncanny accuracy this poetic work struck the nerve of the times and called forth grateful rapture from a whole youthful generation who believed that an interpreter of their innermost life had risen from their own midst—whereas it was a man already forty-two years old who gave them what they sought. And need it be stated that, as an experimental

x

novel, *Steppenwolf* is no less daring than *Ulysses* and *The Counterfeiters?*

For me his life work, with its roots in native German romanticism, for all its occasional strange individualism, its now humorously petulant and now mystically yearning estrangement from the world and the times, belongs to the highest and purest spiritual aspirations and labors of our epoch. Of the literary generation to which I belong I early chose him, who has now attained the Biblical age, as the one nearest and dearest to me and I have followed his growth with a sympathy that sprang as much from our differences as from our similarities. The latter, however, have sometimes astounded me. He has written things—why should I not avow it?— such as *Badegast* and indeed much in *Glasperlenspiel*, especially the great introduction, which I read and feel "as though 'twere part of me."

I also love Hesse the man, his cheerfully thoughtful, roguishly kind ways, the beautiful, deep look of his, alas, ailing eyes, whose blue illuminates the sharp-cut face of an old Swabian peasant. It was only fourteen years ago that I first came to know him intimately when, suffering from the first shock of losing my country, my house and my hearth, I was often with him in his beautiful house and garden in the Ticino. How I envied him in those days!—not alone for his security in a free country, but most of all for the degree of hard-won spiritual freedom by which he surpassed me, for his philosophical detachment from all German politics. There was nothing more comforting, more healing in those confused days than his conversation.

For a decade and more I have been urging that his work be crowned with the Swedish world prize for literature. It would not have come too soon in his sixtieth year, and the choice of a naturalized Swiss citizen would have been a witty way out at a time when Hitler (on account of Ossietzky) had forbidden the acceptance of the prize to all Germans forevermore. But there is much appropriateness in the honor now, too, when the seventy-year-old author has himself crowned his already rich work with something sublime, his great novel of education. This prize carries around the world a name that hitherto has not received proper attention in all countries and it could not fail to enhance the renown of this name in America as well, to arouse the interest of publishers and public. It is a delight for me to write a sympathetic foreword of warm commendation to this American edition of *Demian*, the stirring prose-poem, written in his vigorous middle years. A small volume; but it is often books of small size that exert the greatest dynamic power—take for example *Werther* to which, in regard to its effectiveness in Germany, *Demian* bears a distant resemblance. The author must have had a very lively sense of the suprapersonal validity of his creation

as is proved by the intentional ambiguity of the subtitle
"The Story of a Youth" which may be taken to apply
to a whole young generation as well as to an individual.
This feeling is demonstrated too by the fact that it
was this particular book which Hesse did not wish to
have appear over his own name which was already
known and typed. Instead he had the pseudonym
Sinclair—a name selected from the Hoelderlin circle—
printed on the jacket and for a long time carefully concealed his authorship. I wrote at that time to his pub-
lisher, who was also mine, S. Fischer in Berlin, and
urgently asked him for particulars about this striking
book and who "Sinclair" might be. The old man lied
loyally: he had received the manuscript from Switzer-
land through a third person. Nevertheless the truth
slowly became known, partly through critical analysis of
the style, but also through indiscretions. The tenth edition, however, was the first to bear Hesse's name.

Toward the end of the book (the time is 1914) Demian says to his friend Sinclair: "There will be
war. . . . But you will see, Sinclair, that this is just the
beginning. Perhaps it will become a great war, a very
great war. But even that is just the beginning. The
new is beginning and for those who cling to the old the
new will be horrible. What will you do?"

The right answer would be: "Assist the new without
sacrificing the old." The best servitors of the new—

FOREWORD

Hesse is an example—may be those who know and love the old and carry it over into the new.

THOMAS MANN

Pacific Palisades, California
April 18, 1947

CONTENTS

THE STORY OF
EMIL SINCLAIR'S YOUTH

I wanted only to try to live in obedience to the prompt-ings which came from my true self. Why was that so very difficult?

In order to tell my story, I must begin far back. If it were possible, I should have to go back much further still, to the earliest years of my childhood, and even beyond, to my distant ancestry.

Authors, in writing novels, usually act as if they were God, and could, by a broadness of perception, compre-hend and present any human story as if God were tell-ing it to Himself without veiling anything, and with all the essential details. That I cannot do, any more than can the authors themselves. But I attach more im-portance to my story than can any other writer to his: because it is my own, and it is the story of a human being—not that of an invented, possible, ideal or other-wise, non-existent creature, but that of a real, unique, living man. What that is, a real living man, one certainly knows less today than ever. For men are shot down in heaps—men, of whom each one is a precious, unique experiment of nature. If we were nothing more than individuals, we could actually be put out of the world entirely with a musket-ball, and in that case there would be no more sense in relating stories. But each man is not only himself, he is also the unique, quite special, and in every case the important and remarkable point where the world's phenomena converge, in a certain manner, never again to be repeated. For that reason the history of everyone is important, eternal, divine. For that reason every man, so long as he lives at all and carries out the will of nature, is wonderful and worthy of every attention. In everyone has the spirit taken shape, in everyone creation suffers, in everyone is a redeemer crucified.

Few today know what man is. Many feel it, and for that reason die the easier, as I shall die the easier, when I have finished my story.

I must not call myself one who knows. I was a seeker and am still, but I seek no more in the stars or in books; I am beginning to listen to the promptings of those instincts which are coursing in my very blood. My story is not pleasant, it is not sweet and harmonious like the fictitious stories. It smacks of nonsense and perplexity, of madness and dreams, like the lives of all men who do not wish to delude themselves any longer.

The life of everyone is a way to himself, the search for a road, the indication of a path. No man has ever yet attained to self-realization; yet he strives thereafter, one

2

ploddingly, another with less effort, each as best he can. Each one carries the remains of his birth, slime and eggshells of a primeval world, with him to the end. Many a one will remain a frog, a lizard, an ant. Many a one is top-part man and bottom-part fish. But everyone is a projection of nature into manhood. To us all the same origin is common, our mothers—we all come out of the womb. But each of us—an experiment, one of nature's litter, strives after his own ends. We can understand one another; but each one is able to explain only himself.

Chapter 1

TWO WORLDS

I WILL BEGIN my story with an event of the time when I was ten or eleven years old and went to the Latin school of our little town. Much of the old-time fragrance is wafted back to me, but my sensations are not unmixed, as I pass in review my memories—dark streets and bright houses and towers, the striking of clocks and the features of men, comfortable and homely rooms, rooms full of secrecy and dread of ghosts. I sense again the atmosphere of cozy warmth, of rabbits and servant-girls, of household remedies and dried fruit. Two worlds passed there one through the other. From two poles came forth day and night.

The one world was my home, but it was even narrower than that, for it really comprised only my parents. This world was for the most part very well known to me; it meant mother and father, love and severity, good example and school. It was a world of subdued luster, of clarity and cleanliness; here were tender friendly words, washed hands, clean clothes and good manners. Here the morning hymn was sung, and Christmas was kept.

4

In this world were straight lines and paths which led into the future; here were duty and guilt, evil conscience and confession, pardon and good resolutions, love and adoration, Bible texts and wisdom. To this world our future had to belong, it had to be crystal-pure, beautiful and well ordered.

The other world, however, began right in the midst of our own household, and was entirely different, had another odor, another manner of speech and made different promises and demands. In this second world were servant-girls and workmen, ghost stories and breath of scandal. There was a gaily colored flood of monstrous, tempting, terrible, enigmatical goings-on, things such as the slaughter house and prison, drunken men and scolding women, cows in birth-throes, plunging horses, tales of burglaries, murders, suicides. All these beautiful and dreadful, wild and cruel things were round about, in the next street, in the next house. Policemen and tramps passed to and fro, drunken men beat their wives, crowds of young girls flowed out of factories in the evening, old women were able to bewitch you and make you ill, robbers dwelt in the wood, incendiaries were rounded up by mounted policemen—everywhere seethed and reeked this second, passionate world, everywhere, except in our rooms, where mother and father were. And that was a good thing. It was wonderful that here in our house there were peace, order and repose, duty and a good conscience, pardon and

5

love—and wonderful that there were also all the other things, all that was loud and shrill, sinister and violent, yet from which one could escape with one bound to mother.

And the oddest thing was, how closely the two worlds bordered each other, how near they both were! For instance, our servant Lina, as she sat by the sitting-room door at evening prayers, and sang the hymn with her bright voice, her freshly washed hands laid on her smoothed-out apron, belonged absolutely to father and mother, to us, to what was bright and proper. Immediately after, in the kitchen or in the woodshed, when she was telling me the tale of the headless dwarf, or when she quarreled with the women of the neighborhood in the little butcher's shop, then she was another person, belonged to the other world, and was enveloped in mystery. It was the same with everything and everyone, especially with myself. To be sure, I belonged to the bright, respectable world, I was my parents' child, but the other world was present in everything I saw and heard, and I also lived in it, although it was often strange and foreign to me, although one had there regularly a bad conscience and anxiety. Sometimes I even liked to live in the forbidden world best, and often the homecoming into the brightness—however necessary and good it might be—seemed almost like a return to something less beautiful, to something more uninteresting and desolate. At times I realized this: my

6

aim in life was to grow up like my father and mother, as bright and pure, as systematic and superior. But the road to attainment was long, you had to go to school and study and pass tests and examinations. The road led past the other dark world and through it, and it was not improbable that you would remain there and be buried in it. There were stories of prodigal sons to whom that had happened—I was passionately fond of reading them. There the return home to father and to the respectable world was always so liberating and so sublime, I quite felt that this alone was right and good and desirable. But still that part of the stories which dealt with the wicked and profligate was by far the most alluring, and if one had been allowed to acknowledge it openly, it was really often a great pity that the prodigal repented and was redeemed. But one did not say that, nor did one actually think· it. It was only present somehow or other as a presentiment or a possibility, deep down in one's feelings. When I pictured the devil to myself, I could quite well imagine him down below in the street, openly or in disguise, or at the annual fair or in the public house, but I could never imagine him with us at home.

My sisters also belonged to the bright world. It often seemed to me that they approached more nearly to father and mother; that they were better and nicer mannered than myself, without so many faults. They had their failings, they were naughty, but that did not seem to me to be deep-rooted. It was not the same as for me, for whom the contact with evil was strong and painful, and the dark world so much nearer. My sisters, like my parents, were to be treated with regard and respect. If you had had a quarrel with them, your own conscience accused you afterwards as the wrongdoer and the cause of the squabble, as the one who had to beg pardon. For in opposing my sisters I offended my parents, the representatives of goodness and law. There were secrets which I would much sooner have shared with the most depraved street urchins than with my sisters. On good, bright days when I had a good conscience, it was often delightful to play with my sisters, to be gentle and nice to them, and to see myself under a halo of goodness. That was how it must be if you were an angel! That was the most sublime thing we knew, to be an angel, surrounded by sweet sounds and fragrance like Christmas and happiness. But, oh, how seldom were such days and hours perfect! Often when we were playing one of the nice, harmless, proper games I was so vehement and impetuous, and I so annoyed my sisters that we quarreled and were unhappy. Then when I was carried away by anger I did and said things, the wickedness of which I felt deep and burning within me, even while I was doing and saying them. Then came sad, dark hours of remorse and contrition, the painful moment when I begged pardon, then again a beam of light, a peaceful, grateful happiness without discord, for minutes or hours.

I used to go to the Latin school. The sons of the mayor and of the head forester were in my class and sometimes used to come to our house. They were wild boys, but still they belonged to the world of goodness and of propriety. In spite of that I had close relations with neighbors' boys, children of the public school, whom in general we despised. With one of these I must begin my story.

One half-holiday—I was little more than ten at the time—I went out with two boys of the neighborhood. A public-school boy of about thirteen years joined our party; he was bigger than we were, a coarse and robust fellow, the son of a tailor. His father was a drunkard, and the whole family had a bad reputation. I knew Frank Kromer well, I was afraid of him, and was very much displeased when he joined us. He had already acquired manly ways, and imitated the gait and manner of speech of the young factory hands. Under his leadership we stepped down to the bank of the stream and hid ourselves from the world under the first arch of the bridge. The little bank between the vaulted bridge wall and the sluggishly flowing water was composed of nothing but trash, of broken china and garbage, of twisted bundles of rusty iron wire and other rubbish. You sometimes found there useful things. We had to search the stretch under Frank Kromer's direction and show him what we found. He then either kept it himself or threw it away into the water. He bid us note whether the things were of lead, brass or tin. Everything we found of this description he kept for himself, as well as an old horn comb. I felt very uneasy in his company, not because I knew that father would have forbidden our playing together had he known of it, but through fear of Frank himself. I was glad that he treated me like the others. He commanded and we obeyed; it seemed habitual to me, although that was the first time I was with him.

At last we sat down. Frank spat into the water and looked like a full-grown man; he spat through a gap in his teeth, directing the sputum in any direction he wished. He began a conversation, and the boys vied with one another in bragging of schoolboy exploits and pranks. I was silent, and yet, if I said nothing, I was afraid of calling attention to myself and inciting Kromer's anger against me. My two comrades had from the beginning turned their backs on me, and had sided with him; I was a stranger among them, and I felt my clothes and manner to be a provocation. It was impossible that Frank should like me, a Latin schoolboy and the son of a gentleman, and the other two, I felt, as soon as it came to the point, would disown me and leave me in the lurch.

At last, through mere fright, I also began to relate a story. I invented a long narration of theft, of which I made myself the hero. In a garden by the mill on the corner, I recounted, I had one night with the help of a friend stolen a whole sack of apples, and those none of the ordinary sorts, but russets and golden pippins, the very best. In the danger of the moment I had recourse to the telling of this story, which I invented easily and recounted readily. In order not to have to finish off immediately, and so perhaps be led from bad to worse, I gave full scope to my inventive powers. One of us, I continued, always had to stand sentinel, while the other was throwing down apples from the tree, and the sack had become so heavy that at last we had to open it again and leave half the apples behind; but we returned at the end of half an hour and took the rest away with us.

I hoped at the end to gain some little applause, I had warmed to my work and had let myself go in my narration. The two small boys waited quiet and expectant, but Frank Kromer looked at me penetratingly through half-closed eyes and asked me in a threatening tone:

"Is that true?"

"Yes," I said.

"Really and truly?"

"Yes, really and truly," I asserted defiantly, though inwardly I was stifling through fear.

"Can you swear to it?"

I was terribly frightened, but I answered without hesitation: "Yes."

"Then say: 'I swear by God and all that's holy'!"

I said: "I swear by God and all that's holy!"

"Aw, gwan!" said he and turned away.

I thought that everything was now all right, and was glad when he got up and made for the town. When we were on the bridge I said timidly that I must now go home. "Don't be in such a hurry," laughed Frank, "we both go the same way." He dawdled on, and I dared not tear myself away, especially as he was actually taking the road to our house. As we arrived, I looked at the heavy brass-knocker, the sun on the window and the curtains in my mother's room, and I breathed a sigh of relief. Home at last! What a blessing it was to be at home again, to return to the brightness and peace of the family circle!

As I quickly opened the door and slipped inside, ready to shut it behind me, Frank Kromer forced his way in as well. He stood beside me in the cool, dark stone corridor which was only lighted from the courtyard, held me by the arm and said softly: "Not so fast, you!"

Terrified, I looked at him. His grip on my arm was one of iron. I tried to think what he had in his mind, whether he was going to maltreat me. I wondered, if I should scream, whether anyone would come down quickly enough to save me. But I gave up the idea.

"What's the matter?" I asked. "What d'you want?"

"Nothing much. I only want to ask you something—something the others needn't hear."

"Well, what do you want me to tell you? I must go upstairs, you know."

"You know, don't you, whose orchard that is by the mill on the corner?" said Frank softly.

"No, I don't know; I think it's the miller's."

Frank had wound his arm round me, and he drew me quite close to him, so that I had to look up directly into his face. His look boded ill, he smiled maliciously, and his face was full of cruelty and power.

"Now, kid, I can tell you whose the garden is. I have known for a long time that the apples had been stolen, and I also know that the man said he would give two marks to anyone who would tell him who stole the fruit."

"Good heavens!" I exclaimed. "But you won't tell him anything?" I felt it was useless to appeal to his sense of honor. He came from the other world; for him betrayal was no crime. I felt that for a certainty. In these matters people from the "other" world were not like us.

"Say nothing?" laughed Kromer. "Look here, my friend, d'you think I am minting money and can make two shilling pieces myself? I'm a poor chap, and I haven't got a rich father like yours, and when I get the chance of earning two shillings I must take it. He might even give me more."

Suddenly he let me go free. Our house no longer gave me an impression of peace and safety, the world fell to pieces around me. He would report me as a criminal, my father would be told, perhaps even the police might come for me. The terror of utter chaos menaced me, all that was ugly and dangerous was aligned against me. The fact that I had not stolen at all did not count in the least. I had sworn to it besides. Oh, dear! Oh, dear!

I burst into tears. I felt I must buy myself off. Despairingly I searched all my pockets. Not an apple, not a penknife, absolutely nothing. All at once I thought of my watch. It was an old silver one which wouldn't go. I wore it for no special reason. It came down to me from my grandmother. I drew it out quickly.

"Kromer," I said, "listen, you mustn't give me away, that wouldn't be nice of you. Look here, I will give you my watch; I haven't anything else, worse luck! You can have it, it's a silver one; the mechanism is good, there is one little thing wrong, that's all, it needs repairing."

He smiled and took the watch in his big hand. I looked at his hand and felt how coarse and hostile it was, how it grasped at my life and peace.

"It's silver," I said, timidly.

"I wouldn't give a straw for your silver and your old watch!" he said with deep scorn. "Get it repaired yourself!"

"But, Frank," I exclaimed, quivering with fear lest he should go away. "Wait a minute. Do take the watch! It's really silver, really and truly. And I haven't got anything else." He gave me a cold and scornful look.

"Very well, then, you know who I am going to; or I can tell the police. I know the sergeant very well."

He turned to go. I held him back by the sleeve. I could not let that happen. I would much rather have died than bear all that would take place if he went away like that.

"Frank," I implored, hoarse with emotion, "please don't do anything silly! Tell me it's only a joke, isn't it?"

"Oh, yes, a joke, but it might cost you dear."

"Do tell me, Frank, what to do. I'll do anything!" He examined me critically through his screwed-up eyes and laughed again.

"Don't be silly," he said with affected affability. "You know as well as I do. I've got the chance of earning a couple of marks, and I'm not such a rich fellow that I can afford to throw it away, you know that well enough. But you're rich, why, you've even got a watch. You need only give me just two marks and everything will be all right."

I understood his logic. But two marks! For me that was as much, and just as unobtainable, as ten, a hundred, as a thousand marks. I had no money. There was a money box that my mother kept for me, with a couple

15

of ten and five pfennig pieces inside which I received from my uncle when he paid us a visit, or from similar sources. I had nothing else. At that age I received no pocket-money at all.

"I have nothing," I said sadly. "I have no money at all. But I'll give you everything I have. I've got a book about red Indians, and also soldiers, and a compass. I'll get that for you."

But Kromer only screwed up his evil mouth, and spat on the ground.

"Quit your jawing," he said commandingly. "You can keep your old trash yourself. A compass! Don't make me angry, d'you hear? and hand over the money!"

"But I haven't any. I never get money. I can't help it."

"Very well, then, you'll bring me the two marks in the morning. I shall wait for you in the market after school. That's all. If you don't bring any money, look out!"

"Yes; but where shall I get it, then? Good Lord! if I haven't any—"

"There's enough money in your house. That's your business. Tomorrow after school, then. And I tell you: If you don't bring it—"

His eyes darted a terrible look at me, he spat again and vanished like a shadow.

I could not go upstairs. My life was ruined. I wondered if I should run away and never come back, or go and drown myself. But these thoughts were not clearly formulated. I sat crouched in the dark on the bottom step and I surrendered myself to my misfortune. There Lina found me in tears as she came down with a basket to get wood.

I begged her to say nothing on her return and I went up. My father's hat and my mother's sunshade hung on the rack near the glass door. All these things reminded me of home and tenderness, my heart went out to them imploringly and, grateful for their existence, I felt like the prodigal son when he looked into his old homely room and sensed its familiar atmosphere. All this, the bright father-and-mother world, was mine no longer, and I was buried deeply and guiltily in the strange flood, ensnared in sinful adventures, beset by enemies and dangers, menaced by shame and terror. The hat and sunshade, the good old sandstone floor, the big picture over the hall cupboard, and the voice of my elder sister in the living-room, all this was dearer and more precious to me than ever, but it was no longer consolation and secure possession. All of it was now a reproach. All this belonged to me no more, I could share no more in its cheerfulness and peace. I carried mud on my shoes that I could not wipe off on the mat, I brought shadows in with me, of which the home-world had no knowledge. How many secrets had I already had, how many cares— but that was play, a mere nothing compared with what I was bringing in with me that day.

Fate was overtaking me, hands were stretched out after me, from which even my mother could not protect me, of which she was to be allowed no knowledge. It was all the same, whether my offense was thieving, or a lie (had I not taken a false oath by God?). My sin was not this or that, I had tendered my hand to the devil. Why did I follow him? Why had I obeyed Kromer, more than ever I did my father? Why had I falsely invented the story of the theft? Why had I plumed myself on having committed a crime, as if it had been a deed of heroism? Now the devil had me by the hand, now the evil one was pursuing me.

For a moment I felt no further dread of the morrow, but I had the terrible certainty that my way was leading me further and further downhill and into the darkness. I realized clearly that from my wrongdoing other wrongdoings must result, that the greetings and kisses I gave to my parents would be a lie, that a secret destiny I should have to conceal hung over me.

For an instant confidence and hope came to me like a lightning flash as I gazed at my father's hat. I would tell him everything, would accept his judgment and the punishment he might mete out; he would be my confidant and would save me. Confession was all that would be necessary, as I had made so many confessions before —a difficult bitter hour, a serious, remorseful plea for forgiveness.

How sweetly that sounded! How tempting that was!

But nothing came of it. I knew that I should not do it. I knew that I had now a secret, that I was burdened with guilt for which I myself would have to bear the responsibility alone. Perhaps I was at this very moment at the cross-roads, perhaps from this hour henceforth I should have to belong to the wicked, forever share secrets with the bad, depend on them, obey them, and become as one of themselves. I had pretended to be a man and a hero, now I had to take the consequences.

I was glad that my father, as he entered, found fault with my wet boots. It diverted his attention from something worse, and I allowed myself to suffer his reproach, secretly thinking of the other. That gave birth to a peculiar new feeling in me, an evil cutting feeling like a barbed hook. I felt superior to my father! I felt, for an instant's duration, a certain scorn of his ignorance; his scolding over the wet boots seemed to me petty. "If you only knew!" I thought, and looked upon myself as a criminal who is being tried for having stolen a loaf of bread, while he ought to confess to having committed murder. It was an ugly and repugnant feeling, yet strong and not without a certain charm, and it chained me to my secret and my guilt more securely than anything else. Perhaps Kromer has already gone to the police and given me away, I thought, and a storm is threatening to break over my head, while here I am looked upon as a mere child!

This was the important and permanent element of the

19

whole event up to this point of my narration. It was the first cleft in the sacredness of parenthood, it was the first split in the pillar on which my childhood had reposed, and which everyone must overthrow, before he can attain to self-realization. The inward, fundamental basis of our destiny is built up from these events, which no outsider observes. Such a split or cleft grows together again, heals up and is forgotten, but in the most secret chamber of the soul it continues to live and bleed.

I myself felt immediate terror in the presence of this new feeling, I would have liked to embrace my father's feet there and then, to beg his forgiveness. But one cannot beg pardon for something fundamental, and a child knows and feels that as well and as deeply as any adult.

I felt the need to think over the affair and to consider ways and means for the morrow; but I did not get around to it. My whole evening was taken up solely in accustoming myself to the changed atmosphere of our living-room. Clock and table, Bible and looking-glass, bookcase and pictures seemed all to be saying good-by to me. With freezing heart I had to stand by and watch my world, the good happy time of my life, sever itself from me, to be relegated to the past. I was forced to realize that I was being held fast to new sucking roots in the darkness of the unfamiliar world outside. For the first time I tasted death, and death tasted bitter, for it is birth, with the terror and fear of a formidable renewal.

I was glad to be lying at last in bed. But first I had

passed through purgatory in the form of evening prayers, and we had sung a hymn, one of my favorite ones. Alas! I did not join in, and each note was gall and poison for me. I did not join in the common prayer, either, when my father gave the blessing, and when he finished: "Be with us all!" I tore myself convulsively from the circle. The grace of God was with them all, but with me no longer. Cold and very tired, I went away.

After I had lain awhile in bed, wrapped around in warmth and safety, my troubled heart strayed back once again, and fluttered uneasily in the past. Mother had wished me good-night, as she always did, her step sounded yet in the room, the light of her candle gleamed through the crack in the door. Now, I thought, now she will come back again—she has felt my need, she will give me a kiss and will ask, in tones kind and full of promise, what is the matter. Then I can weep, the lump in my throat will melt away, I will throw my arms about her and will tell her, and everything will be right—I shall be saved! And when the crack in the door had become dark again I still listened for a while and thought—she must come, she must.

Then I came back to reality, and looked my enemy in the face. I saw him clearly, he had one eye closed, his mouth laughed uncouthly. While I gazed at him and the inevitable gnawed at my heart, he became bigger and more ugly, and his wicked eye lit up devilishly. He

21

was close beside me, until I dropped off to sleep. But I did not dream of him, nor of the day's events. I dreamed instead that we were in a boat, my parents, my sisters and I, lapped in peace and the brightness of a holiday. I woke up in the middle of the night, with the after-taste of bliss. I still saw the white summer dresses of my sisters glistening in the sun, and then fell from my paradise back to reality, and the enemy with the wicked eye stood opposite me.

I looked ill when mother came in quickly in the morning and told me how late it was and wanted to know why I was still in bed, and when she asked what was the matter with me, I vomited.

But I seemed to have gained a point. I rather liked to be somewhat ill and to be allowed to spend the morn-ing in bed drinking camomile tea, to listen to mother clearing up in the next room, and to hear Lina outside in the corridor opening the door to the butcher. To stay away from morning school was rather like a fairy-story, and the sun which played in the room was not the same you saw through the green curtains at school. But today all this had lost its charm for me. It had a false ring about it.

If I had died! But I was only slightly ill, as I had often been before, and nothing was gained by that. It pre-vented me from going to school, but it did not protect me in any way from Kromer, who would be waiting for me in the market at eleven o'clock. And mother's friend-

liness was this time without comfort; it was burden-
some and painful. I soon pretended to be asleep again,
and thought the matter over, but all to no purpose—I
had to be in the market at eleven o'clock. For that
reason I got up at ten, and said that I was better. As
usual in such cases I was told that either I must go back
to bed or go to school in the afternoon. I said I would
rather go to school. I had formed a plan.

I dared not go to Kromer without money. I had to
get possession of the little savings-box which belonged
to me. There was not enough money in it, far from
enough, I knew; but it was still a little, and something
told me that a little was better than nothing; for at least
Kromer had to be appeased.

I felt horrible as I crept in my socks into my mother's
room and took my box from her writing table; but it
was not so horrible as the previous day's experience. My
heart beat so fast I nearly died, and it was no better
when I found, at the first look, down below on the stairs,
that the box was locked. It was easy to break it open, it
was only necessary to cut through a thin plate of tin;
but the action caused me pain, for only in doing this
was I committing theft. Up to then I had only taken
lumps of sugar and fruit on the sly. Now I had stolen
something, although it was my own money. I realized I
had taken a step nearer Kromer and his world, that I
was slipping gradually downwards—and I adopted an
attitude of defiance. The devil could run away with me

if he liked, there was no way out. I anxiously counted the money, it had sounded so much in the box, now in my hand it was miserably little. There were sixty-five pfennigs. I hid the box in the basement, held the money in my closed fist and went out of the house, with a feeling different from any with which I had ever left the portal before. Someone called to me from above, I thought, but I went quickly on my way.

There was still plenty of time. I sneaked by a roundabout way through the streets of a changed town, beneath clouds I had never seen before, by houses which seemed to spy on me, and people who suspected me. On the way I recollected that one of my school friends had once found a thaler in the cattle market. I would have liked to pray to God to work a miracle and allow me to make such a treasure-trove. But I had no longer the right to pray. And even then the box would not be made whole again.

Frank Kromer saw me in the distance. However, he came along very slowly and seemed not to be looking out for me. As he approached me he beckoned me commandingly to follow. He passed on tranquilly, without once looking round, went down Straw Street and over the bridge, and stopped on the outskirts of the town in front of a new building. No one was working there, the walls stood bare, without doors or windows. Kromer looked round and then went through the doorway. I followed him. He stepped behind the wall, beckoned to me and stretched out his hand.

"That makes sixty-five pfennigs," he said and looked at me.

"Yes," I said timidly. "That's all I have—it's too little, I know, but it's all. I haven't any more."

"I thought you were cleverer than that," he exclaimed, blaming me in what were almost mild terms. "Between men of honor there must be honest dealing. I will not take anything from you, except what is right. You know that. Take your pfennigs back, there! The other—you know who—doesn't try to beat me down. He pays."

"But I have absolutely nothing else. That was my money-box."

"That's your affair. But I don't want to make you unhappy. You still owe me one mark thirty-five pfennig. When can I have it?"

"Oh, you will soon have it, certainly, Kromer. I don't know yet—perhaps tomorrow, or the day after, I shall have some more. You understand that I can't tell my father, don't you?"

"That's no concern of mine. I don't want to harm you. If I liked, I could get the money before noon, you see, and I'm poor. You wear nice clothes, and you get something better to eat for dinner than I do. But I won't say anything. I am willing to wait a few days. The day after tomorrow, in the afternoon, I will whistle for you, then you will bring it along. You can recognize my whistle?"

He gave me a whistle that I had often heard before. "Yes," I said, "I know it."

He went away, as if I didn't belong to him. It had been only a transaction between us, nothing further.

Even today, I believe, Kromer's whistle would terrify me if I heard it again suddenly. From then on I heard it often. It seemed I heard it continually and always. No place, no game, no work, no idea in which this whistle would not sound. I was dependent on it, it was now the messenger of my fate. On mild, glowing autumn afternoons I was often in our little flower garden, which I loved dearly. A peculiar impulse made me take up again boyish games which I had played formerly. I played, as it were, that I was a boy who was younger than I, who was still good and free, innocent and secure. But in the middle of the game, always expected and yet always terribly disturbing and surprising sounded Kromer's whistle, destroying the picture my imagination had painted.

Then I had to go, I had to follow my tormentor to evil and ugly places, had to render an account and let myself be dunned. The whole business may have lasted a few weeks, but it seemed to me like a year, or an eternity. I seldom had money—a five or ten pfennig piece stolen from the kitchen table when Lina left the market basket standing there. Each time I was blamed by

Kromer, and heaped with abuse; it was I who deceived him and kept back what was his due, it was I who robbed him and made him unhappy! Seldom in life has need so oppressed me, seldom have I felt a greater helplessness, a greater dependence.

I had filled up the savings box with toy money—no one made any enquiries. But that as well could be discovered any day. I was even more afraid of mother than of Kromer's harsh whistle, especially when she stepped up to me softly—was she not going to ask me about the money-box?

As I presented myself to my evil genius several times without money he began to torment and to make use of me after a different fashion. I had to work for him. He had to see to various things for his father. I did that for him or he made me do something more difficult, hop on one leg for ten minutes, or fasten a scrap of paper on to the coat of a passer-by. Many nights these torments realized themselves in my dreams, and I wept and broke out in a cold sweat in my nightmare.

For a time I was ill. I often vomited and felt cold, but at night I lay in a fever, bathed in perspiration. Mother felt that something was wrong and displayed much sympathy on my behalf, but this tortured me because I could not respond by confiding in her.

One evening, after I had already gone to bed, she brought me a piece of chocolate. This action was a souvenir of former years when, if I had been good, I

27

was often rewarded in this way before going off to sleep. Now she stood there and held the piece of chocolate out to me. This so pained me that I could do nothing but shake my head. She asked what was the matter with me and stroked my hair. I could only sob out: "Nothing! nothing! I won't have anything." She put the chocolate on my bed table and went away. When she wished subsequently to question me on the matter I made as if I knew nothing about it. Once she brought the doctor to me, who examined me and prescribed cold ablutions in the morning.

My state at that time was a sort of insanity. I was shy and lived in torment like a ghost in the midst of the well-ordered peace of our house. I had no part in the others' lives, and could seldom, even for as much as an hour, forget my miserable existence. In the presence of my father, who often took me to task in an irritated fashion, I was reserved and wrapped up in myself.

Chapter 2

CAIN

DELIVERANCE from my troubles came from quite an un-
expected quarter, and with it something new entered
into my life, which has up to the present day exercised a
strong influence.

A short time before we had had a new boy at our
Latin school. He was the son of a well-to-do widow
who had moved to our town. He was in mourning and
wore a crape band round his sleeve. His form was above
mine, and he was several years older, but I soon began
to take notice of him, as did all of us. This remarkable
boy impressed one as being much older than he looked.
He made on no one the impression of being a mere
schoolboy. With us childish youngsters he was as distant
and as mature as a man, or rather, as a gentleman. He
was by no means popular, he took no part in the games,
much less in the fooling. It was only the self-conscious
and decided tone which he adopted towards the masters
that pleased the others. His name was Max Demian.

One day it happened, as it occasionally did in our
school, that for some cause or other, another class was
sent into our large schoolroom. It was Demian's form.

We little ones were having Biblical history, the big ones
had to write an essay. While we were having the story
of Cain and Abel knocked into us, I kept looking across
at Demian, whose face fascinated me strangely, and saw
his wise, bright, more than ordinarily strong features
bent attentively and thoughtfully over his task. He did
not look at all like a schoolboy doing an exercise, but
like a research worker solving a problem. I did not find
him really agreeable. On the contrary, I had one or two
little things against him. With me he was too distant
and superior, he was much too provokingly sure of himself, and the expression of his eyes was that of an adult
—which children never like—rather sad with occasional
flashes of scorn. Yet I could not resist looking at him,
whether I liked him or not. But the minute he looked
in my direction I looked away, somewhat frightened. If
today I consider what he looked like as a schoolboy, I
can say that he was in every respect different from the
others, and bore the stamp of a striking personality and
therefore attracted attention. But at the same time he
did everything to prevent himself from being remarked
—he bore and conducted himself like a disguised prince
who finds himself among peasant boys and makes every
effort to appear like them.

He was behind me on the way home from school.
When the others had run on, he overtook me and said:
"Hello!" Even his manner of greeting, although he imi-

tated our schoolboy tone of voice, was polite and like that of a grown-up person.

"Shall we go a little way together?" he questioned in a friendly way. I was flattered and nodded. Then I described to him where I lived.

"Oh, there?" he said laughingly. "I know the house already. There is a remarkable work of art over your door, which interested me at once."

I did not guess immediately to what he was referring, and was astonished that he seemed to know our house better than I did. There was indeed a sort of crest which served as a keystone over the arch of the door, but in course of time it had become faint and had often been painted over. As far as I knew, it had nothing to do with us, or with our family.

"I don't know anything about it," I said timidly. "It's a bird, or something like it; it must be very old. They say that the house at one time belonged to the abbey."

"Very likely," he nodded. "We'll have another good look at it. Such things are often interesting. It is a hawk, I think."

We continued our way. I was considerably embarrassed. Suddenly Demian laughed, as if something funny had struck him.

"Oh, I was present at your lesson," he said with animation. "The story of Cain, who carried the mark on his forehead, was it not? Do you like it?"

Generally I used not to like anything of all the things we had to learn. But I did not dare to say so—it was as though a grown-up person were talking to me. I said I liked the story very much.

Demian tapped me on the shoulder. "No need to pretend with me, old fellow. But the story is really rather remarkable. I think it is much more remarkable than most of the others we get at school. The master didn't say very much about it, only the usual things about God and sin, et cetera. But I believe—" He broke off, smiled, and questioned: "But does it interest you?

"Well," he continued, "I think one can conceive this story of Cain quite differently. Most things we are taught are certainly quite true and right, but one can consider them all from a different standpoint from the master's, and most of them have a much better meaning then. For instance, we can't be quite content with the explanation given us with regard to this fellow Cain and the mark on his forehead. Don't you find it so, too? It certainly might happen that he should kill one of his brothers in a quarrel, it is also possible that he should afterwards be afraid, and have to come down a peg. But that he should be singled out into the bargain with a decoration for his cowardice, which protects him and strikes terror into everyone else, that is really rather odd."

"Certainly," I said, interested. The case began to

interest me. "But how else should one explain the story?" He clapped me on the shoulder.

"Quite simply! The essential fact, and the point of departure of the story, was the sign. Here was a man who had something in his face which terrified other people. They did not dare to molest him, he made a big impression on them, he and his children. Perhaps, or rather certainly, it was not really a sign on his forehead like an office stamp—things are not as simple as that in real life. I would sooner think it was something scarcely perceptible, of a peculiar nature—a little more intelligence and boldness in his look than people were accustomed to. This man had power, other people shrank from him. He had a 'sign.' One could explain that as one wished. And one always wishes what is convenient and agrees with one's opinions. People were afraid of Cain's children, they had a 'sign.' And so they explained the sign not as it really was, a distinction, but as the contrary. The fellows with this sign were said to be peculiar, and they were courageous as well. People with courage and character are always called peculiar by other people. That a race of fearless and peculiar men should rove about was very embarrassing. And so people attached a surname and a story to this race, in order to revenge themselves on it, in order to compensate themselves more or less for all the terror with which it had inspired them. Do you understand?"

"Yes—that means to say, then—that Cain was not at all wicked? And the whole story in the Bible isn't really true?"

"Yes and no. Such ancient, primitive stories are always true, but they have not always been recorded and explained in the proper manner. In short, I mean that Cain was a thundering good fellow, and this story got attached to his name simply because people were afraid of him. The story was merely a report, something people might have set going in a gossiping way, and it was true in so far as Cain and his children did actually wear a sort of 'sign' and were different from most people."

I was much astonished.

"And do you believe then, that the affair of the murder is absolutely untrue?" I asked, much impressed.

"Not at all! It is certainly true. The strong man killed a weak one. One may doubt of course whether it was really his brother or not. It is not important, for, in the end, all men are brothers. A strong man, then, has killed a weak one. Perhaps it was a deed of heroism, perhaps it was not. But in any case the other weak people were terrified, they lamented and complained, and when they were asked: 'Why don't you simply kill him as well?' they did not answer, 'Because we are cowards,' but they said instead: 'You can't. He has a sign. God has singled him out!' The humbug must have arisen something after this style— Oh, I am keeping you from going in. Good-by, then!"

He turned into Old Street and left me alone, more astonished than I had ever been before. Scarcely had he gone when everything that he had said seemed to me quite unbelievable! Cain a noble fellow, Abel a coward! Cain's sign a distinction! It was absurd, it was blasphemous and infamous. What was God's part in the matter? Had he not accepted Abel's sacrifice, did he not love Abel? Demian's story was nonsense! I suspected him of making fun of me and of wishing to mislead me. The devil of a clever fellow, and he could talk, but—well—

Still, I had never thought so much about any of the Biblical or other stories before. And for some time past I had never so completely forgotten Frank Kromer, for hours, for a whole evening. At home I read through the story once again, as it stands in the Bible, short and clear. It was quite foolish to try to find a special, secret meaning. If it had one, every murderer could look upon himself as a favorite of God! No, it was nonsense. But Demian had a nice way of saying such things, so easily and pleasantly, as if everything were self-evident—and then his eyes!

My ideas were certainly a little upset, or rather they were very much confused. I had lived in a bright, clean world, I myself had been a sort of Abel, and now I was so firmly fixed in the other and had sunk so deeply, but really what could I do to help it? What was my position now? A reminiscence glowed in me which for the moment almost took away my breath. I remem-

35

bered that wretched evening, from which my present misery dated, when I looked for an instant into the heart of my father's bright world and despised his wisdom! Then I was Cain and bore the sign; I imagined that it was in no way shameful, but a distinction, and in my wickedness and unhappiness I stood on a higher level than my father, higher than good and pious people.

It was not in such a clear-thinking way that my experience then presented itself to me, but all this was contained therein. It was only a flaming up of feeling, of strange emotions which caused me pain and yet filled me with pride.

When I considered the matter, I saw how strangely Demian had spoken of the fearless and the cowards! How curiously he had explained the mark on Cain's forehead. How singularly his eyes had lit up, those peculiar eyes of a grown person! And indistinctly it shot through my brain: Is not he himself, this Demian, a sort of Cain? Why did he defend him, if he did not feel like him? Why had he this force in his gaze? Why did he speak so scornfully of the "others," of the fearsome, who are really the pious and the well-considered of God?

This thought led me to no definite conclusion. A stone had fallen into the well, and the well was my young soul. And this business with Cain, the murderer and the sign, was for a long, a very long, time the point from which my seekings after knowledge, my doubts and my criticisms took their departure.

I noticed that the other boys also occupied themselves a good deal with Demian. I had not told anyone of his version of the story of Cain, but he appeared to interest the others as well. At least, many rumors concerning the "new boy" became current. If only I still knew all of them, each would help to throw fresh light on him, each would serve to interpret him. I only remember the first rumor was that Demian's mother was very rich. It was also said that she never went to church, nor the son either. Another rumor had it that they were Jews, but they could just as easily have been, in secret, Mohammedans. Furthermore, tales were told of Max Demian's strength. So much was certain, that the strongest boy in his form, who challenged him to a fight, and who at his refusal branded him coward, suffered a terrible humiliation at his hands. Those who were there said that Demian had simply taken him by the nape of the neck with one hand and had brought such a pressure to bear that the boy went white and afterwards crawled away, and that for several days he was unable to use his arm. For a whole evening a rumor even ran that he was dead. For a time everything was asserted and believed, everything that was exciting and wonderful. Then there was a satiety of rumors for a while. A little later new ones circulated, which asserted that Demian had intimate relations with girls and "knew everything."

Meanwhile my affair with Frank Kromer took its inevitable course. I could not get away from him, for although he left me in peace for days together, I was still bound to him. In my dreams he lived as my shadow, and thus my fantasy credited him with actions which he did not, in reality, do; so that in dreams I was absolutely his slave. I lived in these dreams—I was always a deep dreamer—more than in reality. These shadowy conceptions wasted my strength and my life force. I often dreamed, among other things, that Kromer ill-treated me, that he spat on me and knelt on me and, what was worse, that he led me to commit grave crimes—or rather I was not led, but simply forced, through his powerful influence. The most terrible of these dreams, from which I woke up half mad, presented itself as a murderous attack on my father. Kromer whetted a knife and put it in my hand, as we were standing behind the trees of a lane, and lying in wait for someone—whom I knew not; but when someone came along and Kromer through a pressure of the arm informed me that this was the man, whom I was to stab, it turned out to be my father! Then I woke up.

With all these troubles, I still thought a great deal about Cain and Abel, but much less about Demian. It was, strangely enough, in a dream that he first came in contact with me again. I dreamed once more, of assault and ill-treatment which I suffered, but instead of Kromer, this time it was Demian who knelt upon me. And, what was quite new and profoundly impressive, everything that I suffered resistingly and in torment at the hands of Kromer, I suffered willingly from Demian, with a feeling which was composed as much of joy as of fear. I had this dream twice, then Kromer occupied his old position in my thoughts.

For a long time I have not been able to separate what I experienced in these dreams from what I underwent in reality. But in any case my evil relation with Kromer took its course, and was by no means at an end, when I had at last, by petty thefts, paid the boy the sum owed. No, for now he knew of these thefts, as he always asked me where the money came from, and I was more in his hands than ever. He frequently threatened to tell my father everything, and my terror then was scarcely as great as the profound regret that I had not myself done that in the beginning. However, miserable as I was, I did not repent of everything, at least not always, and sometimes felt, I thought, that things could not have helped being as they were. The hand of fate was upon me, and it was useless to want to break away.

I conjecture that my parents suffered not a little in these circumstances. A strange spirit had come over me, I no longer fitted into our community which had been so intimate, and for which I often felt a maddening homesickness, as for a lost paradise. I was treated, particularly by mother, more like a sick person than like a miserable wretch. But the actual state of affairs I was able to observe best in the conduct of my two sisters. It was quite evident from their behavior, which was very considerate and which yet caused me endless pain, that I was a sort of person possessed, who was more to be pitied than blamed for his condition, but yet in whom evil had taken up residence. I felt that I was being prayed for in a different way from formerly, and realized the fruitlessness of these prayers. I often felt burning within me an intense longing for relief, an ardent desire for a full confession, and yet I realized in advance that I should not be able to tell everything to father and mother properly, in explanation of my conduct. I knew that I should be received in a friendly way, that much consideration and compassion would be shown me, but that I should not be completely understood. The whole affair would have been looked upon as a sort of backsliding, whereas it was really the work of destiny.

I know that many people will not believe that a child scarcely eleven years old could feel thus. But I am not relating my affairs for their benefit. My narration is for those who know mankind better. The grown-up person who has learned to convert part of his feelings into thoughts, feels the absence of these ideas in a child, and comes to believe that the experiences are likewise lacking. But they have seldom been so vivid and not often in my life have I suffered as keenly as then.

One rainy day I was ordered by my tormentor to Castle Place, and there I stood, waiting and digging my feet in the wet chestnut leaves, which were still falling regularly from the black, dripping branches. Money I had none, but I had brought with me two pieces of cake that I had stolen in order at least to be able to give Kromer something. I had long since been accustomed to stand about in any odd corner waiting for him often for a very long time, and I put up with the unalterable.

Kromer came at last. That day he did not stay long. He poked me several times in the ribs, laughed, took the cake, and even offered me a moldy cigarette, which however I did not accept. He was more friendly than usual.

"Oh," he said, as he went away, "before I forget— next time you can bring your sister along, the elder one. What's her name? Now tell the truth."

I did not understand, and gave no answer. I only looked at him wonderingly.

"Don't you get me? You must bring your sister along."

"But, Kromer, that won't do. I mustn't do that, and besides she wouldn't come."

I thought this was only another pretext for vexing me. He often did that, requiring me to do something impossible, and so terrifying me. And often, after humiliating me, he would by degrees become more tractable. I then had to buy myself off with money or with some other gift.

41

This time he was quite different. He was really not at all angry at my refusal.

"Well," he said airily, "you'll think about it, won't you? I should like to make your sister's acquaintance. It will not be so difficult. You simply take her out for a walk, and then I come along. Tomorrow I'll whistle for you, and then we can talk more about it."

When he had gone, a glimpse of the meaning of his request dawned on me. I was still quite a child, but I knew by hearsay that boys and girls, when they were somewhat older, did things which were forbidden, things of a secret and scandalous nature. And now I should also have to—it was suddenly quite clear to me how monstrous it was! I immediately resolved never to do that. But I scarcely dared think of what would happen in that case and how Kromer would revenge himself on me. A new torment began, I had not yet been tortured enough.

I walked disconsolately across the empty square, my hands in my pockets. Fresh torments, a new servitude!

Suddenly a fresh, deep voice called to me. I was terrified and began to run on. Someone ran after me, a hand gripped me from behind. It was Max Demian.

I let myself be taken prisoner. I surrendered.

"It's you?" I said uncertainly. "You frightened me so!"

He looked at me, and never had his glance been more like that of an adult, of a superior and penetrating person. For a long time past we had not spoken with one another.

"I am sorry," he said in his courteous and at the same time very determined manner. "But listen, you mustn't let yourself be frightened like that."

"Oh, that can happen sometimes."

"So it appears. But look here: If you shrink like that from someone who hasn't hurt you, then this someone begins to think. It makes him curious, he wonders what can be the matter. This somebody thinks to himself, how awfully frightened you are, and he thinks further: one is only like that when one is terrified. Cowards are always frightened; but I believe you aren't really a coward. Aren't I right? Of course, you aren't a hero either. There are things of which you are afraid. There are also people of whom you are afraid. And that should never be. No one should ever be afraid of other people. You aren't afraid of me? Or are you, perhaps?"

"Oh no, of course not."

"There, you see. But there are people you are afraid of?"

"I don't know . . . let me go, what do you want of me?"

He kept pace with me—I was going quicker with the idea of escaping—I felt his look directed on me from the side.

"Just assume," he began again, "that I mean well with you. In any case you needn't be afraid of me. I would very much like to try an experiment with you—it's funny, and you can learn something that's very useful. Listen: I often practice an art which is called mind-reading. There's no witchcraft in it, but it seems very peculiar if one doesn't know how to do it. You can surprise people very much with it. Well, let us try it. I like you, or I interest myself in you, and I would like to find out what your real feelings are. I have already made the first step towards doing that. I have frightened you—you are, then, easily frightened. There are things and people of which and of whom you are afraid. Why is it? One need be afraid of no one. If you fear somebody then it is due to the fact that he has power over you. For example, you have done something wrong, and the other person knows it—then he has power over you. D'you get me? It's clear, isn't it?"

I looked helplessly into his face, which was serious and prudent as always, and kind as well, but without any tenderness—his features were rather severe. Righteousness or something akin lay therein. I was not conscious of what was happening; he stood like a magician before me.

"Have you understood?" he questioned again.

I nodded. I could not speak.

"I told you mind-reading looked rather strange, but the process is quite natural. I could for example tell you more or less exactly what you thought about me when I once told you the story of Cain and Abel. But that has

44

nothing to do with the matter in hand. I also think it possible that you have dreamed of me. But let's leave that out! You're a clever kid, most of 'em are so stupid. I like talking now and then with a clever fellow whom I can trust. You have no objections, have you?"

"Oh, no! Only I don't understand."

"Let's keep to our old experiment! We have found that: the boy S. is easily frightened—he is afraid of somebody—he apparently shares a secret with this other person, which causes him much disquietude. Is that about right?"

As in a dream I lay under the influence of his voice, of his personality. I only nodded. Was not a voice talking there, which could only come from myself? Which knew all? Which knew all in a better, clearer way than I myself?

Demian gave me a powerful slap on the shoulder.

"That's right then. I thought so. Now just one question more: Do you know the name of the boy who has just gone away?"

I sank back, he had the key to my secret, this secret which twisted back inside me as if it did not want to see the light.

"What sort of a fellow? There was no one there, except myself."

He laughed.

"Don't be afraid to tell me," said he laughingly. "What's his name?"

I whispered: "Do you mean Frank Kromer?"

He nodded contentedly.

"Bravo! You're a smart chap, we shall be good friends yet. But now I must tell you something else: this Kromer, or whatever his name is, is a nasty fellow. His face tells me he's a rascal! What do you think?"

"Oh yes," I sobbed out, "he is nasty, he's a devil! But he mustn't know anything! For God's sake, he mustn't know anything. D'you know him? Does he know you?"

"Don't worry! He's gone, and he doesn't know me—not yet. But I should like to make his acquaintance. He goes to the public school?"

"Yes."

"In which class?"

"In the fifth. But don't say anything to him! Please, don't say anything to him!"

"Don't worry, nothing will happen to you. I suppose you wouldn't like to tell me a little more about this fellow Kromer?"

"I can't! No, let me go!"

He was silent for a while.

"It's a pity," he said, "we might have been able to carry the experiment still further. But I don't want to bother you. You know, don't you, that it is not right of you to be afraid of him? Such fear quite undermines us, you must get rid of it. You must get rid of it, if you want to become a real man. D'you understand?"

"Certainly, you are quite right . . . but it won't do. You don't know . . ."

"You have seen that I know a lot, more than you thought. Do you owe him any money?"

"Yes, I do, but that isn't the essential point. I can't tell, I can't!"

"It won't help matters, then, if I give you the amount you owe him? I could very well let you have it."

"No, no, that is not the point. And please: don't say anything to anybody! Not a word! You are making me miserable!"

"Rely on me, Sinclair. Later you can share your secrets with me."

"Never, never!" I exclaimed vehemently.

"Just as you please. I only mean, perhaps you will tell me something more later on. Only of your own free will, you understand. Surely you don't think I shall act like Kromer?"

"Oh no—but you don't even know anything about it!"

"Absolutely nothing. But I think about it. And I shall never act like Kromer, believe me. Besides, you don't owe me anything."

We remained a long time silent, and I became more tranquil. But Demian's knowledge became more and more of a puzzle to me.

"I'm going home now," he said, and in the rain he drew his coat more closely about him. "I should only like to repeat one thing to you, since we have gone so far in the matter—you ought to get rid of this fellow! If there is nothing else to be done, then kill him! It would impress me and please me, if you were to do that. Besides, I would help you."

I was again terrified. I suddenly remembered the story of Cain. I had an uncanny feeling and I began to cry softly. So much that was weird seemed to surround me.

"All right," Max Demian said, smilingly. "Go home now! We will put things square, although murder would have been the simplest. In such matters the simplest way is always the best. You aren't in good hands, with your friend Kromer."

I came home, and it seemed to me as if I had been away a year. Everything looked different. Between myself and Kromer there now stood something like future freedom, something like hope. I was lonely no longer! And then I realized for the first time how terribly lonely I had been for weeks and weeks. And I immediately recollected what I had on several occasions turned over in my mind: that a confession to my parents would afford me relief and yet would not quite liberate me. Now I had almost confessed, to another, to a stranger, and as if a strong perfume had been wafted to me, sensed the presentiment of salvation!

Still my fear was far from being overcome, and I was

still prepared for long and terrible mental wrestlings with my evil genius. So it was all the more remarkable to me that everything passed off so very secretly and quietly.

Kromer's whistle remained absent from our house for a day, two days, three days, a whole week. I dared not believe my senses, and lay inwardly on the watch, to see whether he would not suddenly stand before me, just at that moment when I should expect him no longer. But he was, and remained, away! Distrustful of my new freedom, I still could not bring myself to believe in it whole-heartedly. Until at last I met Frank Kromer. He was coming down the street, straight in my direction. When he saw me, he drew himself together, twisted his features in a brutal grimace, and turned away without more ado, in order to avoid meeting me.

That was a wonderful moment for me! My enemy ran away from me! My devil was afraid of me! Surprise and joy shook me through and through!

In a few days Demian showed himself once again. He waited for me outside school.

"Hullo," I said.

"Good morning, Sinclair. I only wanted to hear how you're getting on. Kromer leaves you in peace, doesn't he?"

"Did you manage that? But how did you do it? How? I don't understand it. He hasn't come near me."

"Splendid. If he should come again—I don't think he will, but he's a cheeky fellow—then simply tell him to remember Demian."

"But what does it all mean? Have you had a fight with him and thrashed him?"

"No, I'm not so keen on that. I simply talked to him, as I did to you, and I made it clear to him that it is to his own advantage to leave you in peace."

"Oh, but you haven't given him any money?"

"No, kid. You have already tried that way yourself."

I attempted to pump him on the matter, but he disengaged himself. The old, embarrassed feeling concerning him came over me—an odd mixture of gratitude and shyness, of admiration and fear, of affection and inward resistance.

I had the intention of seeing him again soon, and then I wanted to talk more about everything, about the Cain affair as well. But I did not see him. Gratitude is not one of the virtues in which I believe, and to require it of a child would seem to me wrong. So I do not wonder very much at the complete ingratitude which I evinced towards Max Demian. Today I believe positively that I should have been ruined for life if he had not freed me from Kromer's clutches. At that time also I already felt this release as the greatest event of my young life—but I left the deliverer on one side as soon as he had accomplished the miracle.

As I have said, ingratitude seems to me nothing strange. Solely, the lack of curiosity I evinced is odd. How was it possible that I could continue for a single day my quiet mode of life without coming nearer to the secrets with which Demian had brought me in contact? How could I restrain the desire to hear more about Cain, more about Kromer, more about the thought-reading?

It is scarcely comprehensible, and yet it is so. I suddenly saw myself extricated from the demoniacal toils, saw again the world lying bright and cheerful before me. I was no longer subject to paroxysms of fear. The curse was broken, I was no longer a tormented and condemned creature, I was a schoolboy again. My temperament sought to regain its equilibrium and tranquillity as quickly as possible, and so I took pains above all things to put behind me all that had been ugly and menacing, and to forget it. The whole, long story of my guilt, of my terrifying anxiety, slipped from my memory wonderfully quick, apparently without having left behind any scars or impressions whatsoever.

The fact that I likewise tried as quickly to forget my helper and deliverer, I understand today as well. Instinctively my mind turned from the damning recollection of my awful servitude under Kromer, and I sought to recover my former happy, contented mental outlook, to regain that lost paradise which opened once more to me, the bright father-and-mother world, where my sisters dwelt in the fragrant atmosphere of purity, in loving kindness such as God had extended to Abel.

On the very next day after my short conversation with Demian, when I was at last fully convinced of my newly-born freedom and feared no longer a relapse to my condition of slavery, I did what I had so often and so ardently desired to do—I confessed. I went to mother and showed her the little savings-box with the broken lock, filled with toy mark pieces instead of with real money, and I told her how long I had been in the thrall of an evil tormentor, through my own guilt. She did not understand everything, but she saw the money-box, she saw my altered look and heard my changed voice—she felt that I was healed, that I had been restored to her.

And then with lofty feelings I celebrated my readmission into the family, the prodigal son's return home. Mother took me to father, the story was repeated, questions and exclamations of wonder followed in quick succession, both parents stroked my hair and breathed deeply, as in relief from a long oppression. It was all lovely, like the stories I had read, all discords were resolved in a happy ending.

I surrendered myself passionately to this harmonious state of affairs. I could not have enough of the idea that I was again free and trusted by my parents. I was a model boy at home and played more frequently than ever with my sisters. At prayers I sang the dear, old hymns with the blissful feeling of one converted and redeemed. It came straight from my heart, it was no lie this time.

And yet it was not at all as it should have been. And this is the point which alone can truly explain my forgetfulness of Demian. I ought to have made a confession *to him!* The confession would have been less touching and less specious, but for me it would have borne more fruit. I was now clinging fast to my former paradisaical world, I had returned home and had been received in grace. But Demian belonged in no wise to this world, he did not fit into it. He also—in a different way from Kromer —but nevertheless he also was a seducer, he too bound me to the second, evil, bad world, and of this world I never wanted to hear anything more. I could not now, and I did not wish to give up Abel and help to glorify Cain, now when I myself had again become an Abel.

So much for the outward correlation of events. But inwardly it was like this: I had been freed from the hands of Kromer and the devil, but not through my own strength and effort. I had ventured a footing on the paths of the world, and they had been too slippery for me. Now that the grasp of a friendly hand had saved me, I ran back, without another glance round, to mother's lap, to the protecting, godly and tender security of childhood. I made myself younger, more dependent on others, more childlike than I really was. I had to replace my dependence on Kromer by a new one, since

I was powerless to strike out for myself. So I chose, in the blindness of my heart, the dependence on father and mother, on the old, beloved, "bright world," on this world which I knew already was not the sole one. Had I not done this, I should have had to hold to Demian, to entrust myself to him. The fact that I did not, appeared to me then to be due to justifiable distrust of his strange ideas; in reality it was due to nothing else than fear. For Demian would have required more of me than did my parents, much more. By stimulation and exhortation, by scorn and irony he would have tried to make me more independent. Alas, I know that today: nothing in the world is so distasteful to man as to go the way which leads him to himself!

And yet, about half a year later, I could not resist the temptation to ask my father while we were out for a walk, what was to be made of the fact that many people declared Cain to be better than Abel.

He was much surprised, and explained to me that this was a conception by no means novel. It had even emerged in the early Christian era, and had been professed by sects, one of which was called the "Cainites." But naturally this foolish doctrine was nothing else than an attempt of the devil to undermine our belief. For, if one believes that Cain was right and Abel was wrong, then it follows that God has erred, and that the God of the Bible is not the true and only God, but a false one. The Cainites really used to profess and preach something approximating this doctrine; but this heresy vanished from among mankind a long time ago and he wondered the more that a school friend had been able to learn something on the subject. Nevertheless, he earnestly exhorted me not to let these ideas occupy my attention.

Chapter 3

THE THIEF ON THE CROSS

I COULD DESCRIBE scenes of my childhood, spent in peaceful security at the side of father and mother, relate how I passed this period of my life, playing contentedly in the midst of surroundings brightened by love and tenderness. But others have done that. I am only interested in the steps I took in life, in order to attain self-realization. All the pretty resting-places, happy isles and children's paradises, whose charm is not unknown to me, I leave lying behind me in the shimmer of a distant horizon, and I have no desire to set foot there again.

For that reason I will speak, so far as I intend to dwell on the period of my childhood, only of new events which overtook me, of what impelled me forward enabling me to throw off my shackles.

These impulses always came from the "other" world, they always brought fear, coercion and a bad conscience in their train, they were always of a revolutionary tendency and a danger to the peace in which I would willingly have been allowed to remain.

There came the years in which I had to discover anew that there was within me an instinct which had to lie

close and concealed in the bright world of moral sanction. As to every man, the slowly awakening sense of
sex came to me as an enemy and a destroyer, as something forbidden, as seduction and sin. What my curiosity sought to know, what caused me dreams, desire and
fear, the great secret of puberty, that was not at all in
keeping with the guarded happiness of my peaceful
childhood. I did as everyone else. I led the double life
of a child, who is yet a child no longer. My conscious
self lived under the conditions sanctioned at home; it
denied the existence of the new world whose dawn glimmered before me. But I lived as well in dreams, impelled by desires of a secret nature, upon which my conscious self anxiously attempted to build a new fabric, as
the world of my childhood fell in ruins about me. Like
almost all parents, my own did nothing to help the
awakening life-instincts, about which not a syllable was
uttered. They only aided, with untiring care, my hopeless attempts to deny the reality, and to continue my existence in a childlike world which was ever becoming
more unreal and more mendacious. I do not know
whether parents can do much in such a case, and I make
mine no reproach. It was my own affair, to settle my
difficulties and to find my way, and I carried through
the business badly, like most of those who are well
brought up.

Every man passes through this difficulty. For the
average person, this is the point in his life where the

demands of his own life come most in conflict with his surroundings, where the road forward has to be attained through the bitterest fighting. For many people this is the only time in their lives that they experience the sequence of death and rebirth that is our fate, when they become conscious of the slow process of the decay and breaking up of the world of their childhood, when everything beloved of us leaves us, and we suddenly feel the loneliness and deathly cold of the universe around us. And for very many this pitfall is fatal. They cling their whole life long painfully to the irrevocable past, to the dream of a lost paradise, the worst and most deadly of all dreams.

But to return to the story. The sensation and dream pictures in which the close of childhood presented itself to me are not important enough to be described. The important point was that I was once again conscious of the existence of the "dark" world, the "other" world. What Frank Kromer had once been to me, was now present within myself. And so, from the outside as well, the other world once more gained power over me.

Several years had passed since my affair with Kromer. That dramatic and guilty time of my life lay far behind me at that time and seemed to have passed like a quick nightmare into nothingness. Frank Kromer had long since disappeared from my life; I scarcely gave it a moment's thought if I chanced to meet him. But the other important figure in my tragedy, Max Demian, never entirely disappeared from my life. However, for a long time he stood on the far horizon, visible, but not affecting me. Only by degrees he approached me again, and I came once more under the ray of his power and influence.

I will try to recollect what I know of Demian in that period. Perhaps for a year, or longer, I did not have a single conversation with him. I avoided him, and he in no wise forced himself on me. Once or twice, when we met, he nodded to me in friendly greeting. Then it seemed to me at times that there was a note of scorn or ironical reproach in his friendliness, but that might only have been imagination on my part. My relation with him, and the strange influence he had exercised over me, were as if forgotten, by him as well as by me.

I try to recall his face—as I recollect him, I see that I was conscious of his existence after all, and took notice of him. I can see him going to school, alone or with some of the other big boys. I see him walking among them like a stranger, lonely and still like a celestial body, enveloped in a different atmosphere and subject to his own laws. No one liked him, he was intimate with no one, except his mother, and his relations with her did not seem like those of a child, but those of a grown-up person. The masters left him as much as possible in peace. He was a good pupil, but he did not go out of his way to please them. From time to time we heard, in gossip, of a word, a comment or a retort he had made to a

master, and which left nothing to be desired in the way
of blunt challenge or irony.

I call him to mind, as I close my eyes, and I see his
picture emerge. Where was it? Ah, now I have it again.
It was in the street, in front of our house. There one
day I saw him standing, a note book in his hand. I saw
that he was drawing. He was drawing the old crest with
the bird over the door of our house. And I stood at a
window, concealed behind a curtain, and gazed at him.
I saw with astonishment his attentive, cool, bright features turned to the crest, the features of a man, of a research worker, or an artist, superior and full of will-
power, oddly bright and cool, with knowing eyes.

And again I can see him. It was a little later, in the
street; we had come out of school and were all standing
round a horse that had fallen down. It lay, still har-
nessed to the shaft, in front of a peasant's cart, and
sniffed the air pitifully with open nostrils, while blood
flowed from an invisible wound, so that the white dust
in the street darkened as it became slowly saturated. As
I, with a feeling of nausea, turned my gaze away, I saw
Demian's face. He had not pressed forward, he stood
furthest back of all, rather elegant, quite at his ease, as
was proper to him. His gaze seemed to be directed at
the horse's head, and expressed again that deep, quiet,
almost fanatical and yet calm attentiveness. I could not
resist watching him some considerable time, and I remember feeling, though quite unconsciously, that there

was something very peculiar about him. I saw Demian's face, I saw not only that he had not the face of a boy, but that of a man; I saw still more, I thought I saw, or felt, that it was not the face of a man either but something else besides. There seemed to be also something of the woman in his features, and particularly it seemed to me for a moment, not manly or boyish, nor old or young, but somehow or other a thousand years old, not to be measured by time, bearing the stamp of other epochs. Animals could look like that, or trees, or stones—I did not realize that precisely, I did not experience the exact sensation which I, a grown-up person, am now describing, but what I felt then approximated in some way to what I have just related. Perhaps he was beautiful, perhaps he pleased me, perhaps even he was repugnant—I could not then determine. I saw only that he was different from us, he was like an animal, or a spirit, or a picture, I know not what he was like, but he was different, inconceivably different from us all.

My reminiscence tells me nothing more, and perhaps even what has been described has arisen, in part, from later impressions.

Until I was several years older, I did not come into close contact with him again. Contrary to custom, Demian had not been confirmed with the boys of his year, and in consequence fresh rumors concerning him were set afloat. In school they were again saying that he was really a Jew, or no, a heathen, and others pretended to know that he and his mother professed no religion, or that they belonged to a bad sect in mythology. In connection with this I seem to remember that he was suspected of living with his mother as with a mistress. Presumably the facts were that he had been, up to that time, brought up without any denominational creed, and that it was now thought that this might be disadvantageous for his future career. In any case, his mother now decided after all to allow him to be prepared for confirmation, two years later than the boys of his own age. Hence it came about that for months he was my classmate in the confirmation class.

For a time I kept out of his way, I did not want to have anything to do with him; too many mysterious rumors had become attached to his name. But above all things I was worried by a sense of obligation, implanted in me since my affair with Kromer. And just at that time I had enough to do with my own secrets. For the confirmation class coincided with the period when I was definitively enlightened on matters of sex, and in spite of my good will, my interest in the pious instruction was on that account greatly diminished. The things of which the clergyman spoke lay far from me in a still, sacred unreality; they may have been quite beautiful and valuable, but in no way real and stirring, as were in the highest degree, these other things.

The more indifferent I became, under these conditions, to our spiritual instruction, the more was my interest drawn towards Max Demian again. Something or other seemed to unite us. As nearly as I remember it began in class early one morning, while the light was still burning in the schoolroom. The clergyman taking the confirmation class happened to be talking about Cain and Abel. I hardly paid any attention, I was sleepy and scarcely listened. Then with raised voice the clergyman began to speak fervently of Cain's sign. At this moment I felt a sort of contact or exhortation and looking up I saw Demian's face turned toward me from a row of desks in front, with a bright speaking look, which could have expressed scorn as much as seriousness. He looked at me for a moment only, and suddenly I was listening intently to the clergyman's words. I heard him speak of Cain and the mark on his forehead, and suddenly I felt deep within me the knowledge that the story could have a different signification, that it could be looked at from another view, that it was possible to be critical.

From that instant the bond of communication between Demian and myself was again established. And oddly enough, scarcely had this sense of a certain solidarity between us presented itself to my mind, than I saw it transferred as if by magic from the ideal world to the world of space. I did not know whether he had been able to arrange it himself, or whether it was pure chance —at that time I believed firmly in chance—but a few days after I noticed Demian had suddenly changed his place and was now sitting directly in front of me. (I recollect still how pleasant it was, in the midst of the miserable workhouse atmosphere of the overcrowded schoolroom, to sense the delicate, fresh aroma of soap from his neck in the morning.) A few days later he had changed again, and now sat next to me. And there he stayed, occupying the same place through the whole of that winter and spring.

Morning lessons had quite changed. They were no longer sleepy and boring. I looked forward to them. Sometimes we both listened to the clergyman with the greatest attention. A glance from my neighbor would suffice, calling my attention to a strange story or a peculiar text. And another glance from him, a very decided one, acted on me as an admonition, arousing criticism and doubt.

But very often we were bad pupils and heard nothing of the lesson. Demian was always courteous towards masters and schoolfellows. I never saw him commit a schoolboy prank, never heard him laugh out loud or talk in class; he never drew on himself the master's blame. But noiselessly, rather by signs and glances than by whispered words, he knew how to let me share in his own occupations. These were, in part, of a peculiar nature.

For instance, he told me which of the fellows interested him; and in what manner he studied them. He judged many of them with accuracy. He used to say to me before the lesson: "When I signal to you with my thumb, so and so will look round at us, or will scratch his neck, etc." Then during the lesson, when I scarcely gave a thought to what he had told me, Max would attract my attention by suddenly bending his thumb. I would look up quickly at the boy already designated, and every time, as if attached to a wire, the fellow would make the gesture required of him. I bothered Max to try this on the master, but he did not want to do it. But once, when I came into class and told him I had not done my preparation, and that I hoped the clergyman would not question me that day, he helped me. The master looked round for a boy to recite a portion of the catechism, and his roving eye rested on me. He approached me slowly, stretched out his finger in my direction, and already had my name on his lips—when suddenly he became absent-minded or uneasy, put his hand to his collar, stepped up to Demian who looked fixedly into his face. He seemed to want to ask him something but he turned away, to our surprise, coughed a little, and put his question to another boy.

These jokes amused me very much, but only gradually did I notice that my friend frequently played the same game with me. It would happen that on my way home from school I had suddenly the feeling Demian was a little way behind me, and when I turned round, there he was, sure enough.

"Can you really make another person think what you want him to?" I asked him.

He gave me information on the subject readily enough, quietly and pertinently, in his grown-up manner.

"No," he said, "that can't be done. That is to say, one hasn't a free will, even if the parson acts that way. Neither can the other person think as he will, nor can I make him think what I want him to. But you can observe someone well, and then you can say fairly exactly what he thinks or feels; in this way you can generally predict what he will do the moment after. It's quite simple, but people merely do not know it. Naturally it requires practice. To take an example from the butterfly world, there is a certain species of moth, of which the female is much rarer than the male. The moths reproduce like other animals, the male impregnates the female, who then lays the egg. Suppose you have in your possession a female of this type of moth—naturalists have often made the experiment—then the male moths fly in the night to this female, they even make a flight of several hours' duration! Think of it! For many miles around all the males are conscious of the whereabouts of the only female moth in the district. People have tried to explain that, but it is not easy. Moths must have a sense of smell, or something like it, which allows them to pick up and follow an almost imperceptible scent, like a good hound. You understand? There are such things, nature is full of them, and no one can explain them. Now I draw the conclusion that if among this class of moths the females were as abundant as the males, then these latter would not have such a refined sense of smell! They have it simply because they have been trained like that. If an animal or a man concentrates his whole attention and his whole will-power on a certain thing then he attains it. That's all. And it is just the same with what you have asked me. Observe a man sufficiently well, and you will know more about him than he does himself."

It lay on the tip of my tongue to mention the word "mind-reading," and so to remind him of the scene with Kromer, now relegated to such a distant past. But the odd thing between us both was that neither he nor I ever made the slightest reference to the fact that several years ago he had intervened so decisively in my life. It was as if formerly there had been nothing between us, or as if each of us reckoned that the other had forgotten the affair. It even happened once or twice when we were together that we met Frank Kromer in the street, but we exchanged no look, neither did we speak of him.

"But what has that got to do with will-power?" I asked. "You said there was no such thing as free will. And then you said one only had to concentrate one's will on something to be able to attain one's ends. That doesn't agree! If I am not master of my will, then I can't direct it here or there as I wish."

"A good question!" he said, laughing. "You should always ask questions, you must always doubt. But the explanation is very simple. If a moth for instance wants to concentrate his will-power on a star or something like that, he can't do it. Only—he doesn't try. He seeks only what has sense and value for him, satisfies his needs, he gets what he absolutely must have. And it is just there that the unbelievable succeeds—he develops a marvelous sixth sense, that no other animal besides him has! People in our position have more elbow-room, certainly, and more interests than an animal. But even we are confined to a comparatively small space, beyond which we cannot go. To be sure, I can imagine this or that, or make myself believe that I absolutely want to get to the North Pole or somewhere, but I can only carry that out and wish it strongly enough when the desire lies right in myself, when my whole being is really filled with it. As soon as that is the case, as soon as you try to carry out an inward command, then you succeed, then you can harness your will as you would a good nag. If for instance I resolved that our good Mr. Parson shall not wear his spectacles for the future, then that wouldn't work. That is merely play. But when last autumn I had the fixed intention of getting myself moved to another desk, I succeeded. Someone suddenly arrived

who came before me in the alphabet and who up to
then had been ill. Because someone had to make room
for him, it was naturally I who did it, because my willing it had made me ready to seize the opportunity."

"Yes," I said, "that seemed to me very strange at the
time. From the moment we began to get interested in
one another, you managed to get nearer and nearer to
me. But how was that? You did not immediately take a
place next to me; for a few lessons at first you were
sitting in the row of desks in front of me, weren't you?
How did that come about?"

"It was like this. I wasn't quite certain where I
wanted to go when I wished to move from my first
place. I only knew that I wanted to sit further back. It
was my wish to move towards you, but I was not conscious of this at the time. Simultaneously your own will
was working with mine and helped me. It was only
when I sat in front of you that I realized my wish was
only half fulfilled—I noticed that really I had desired
nothing else than to sit next to you."

"But on that occasion no newcomer arrived."

"No, but then I simply did what I wished, and sat
next to you without hesitation. The boy with whom I
changed places was simply surprised, and let me do it
without further say. And the parson indeed noticed
once that a change had taken place—in fact, whenever
he looks at me something worries him secretly. That is
to say, he knows my name is Demian, and that some-

thing must be wrong that I, whose initial is D, am sitting back there among the S's! But that does not penetrate his consciousness because my will is against it, because I prevent him again and again from becoming conscious of it. He notices now and then that something is wrong. He looks at me and begins to study the question, the good fellow. But I have a simple means at my disposal. I look at him very, very fixedly in the eyes. Hardly anyone can bear that. They always get restive. If you want to get something out of a person, and you fix him unexpectedly with your eyes, and if he doesn't get restive, then give it up! You won't get anything out of him, ever! But that happens seldom. I know only one single person with whom this trick won't help me."

"Who is that?" I asked quickly.

He looked at me, with eyes somewhat closed; as his fashion was when he meditated. Then he looked away and gave no answer, and in spite of my lively curiosity I could not bring myself to repeat the question.

But I believe he was referring to his mother. He seemed to live on very intimate terms with her, but he never spoke about her, never invited me to his house. I scarcely knew what his mother looked like.

Several times I attempted to imitate his example by concentrating my will-power on something so firmly that I would have to attain it. I had desires which seemed to me sufficiently pressing. But nothing came of it. I could not bring myself to talk matters over with Demian. I should not have been able to make him understand what I wanted. He did not ask, either.

My faith in matters of religion had meanwhile suffered many a breach. Yet in my manner of thinking, which was entirely under the influence of Demian, I was to be distinguished from those of my schoolfellows who professed an entire disbelief. There were a few such who let occasional phrases be overheard, to the effect that it was laughable and unworthy of man's dignity to believe in a God, and that stories such as those of the Trinity and the immaculate conception of the Virgin Mary were simply a joke. It was disgraceful, they said, that such rubbish was peddled about today. This was by no means my way of thinking. Even where I had doubts, the whole experience of my childhood taught me to believe in the efficacy of a godly life such as that led by my parents, which I knew to be neither contemptible nor hypocritical. On the contrary, now as before, I had the greatest reverence for the spirit of religion. Only Demian had accustomed me to consider and explain the stories and articles of belief from a more liberal and more personal point of view, a point of view in which fantasy and imagination had their share. At least, I always took great pleasure and enjoyment in the interpretations he suggested to me. To be sure much seemed to me too crude; such as the affair of Cain. And once, during the preparation for confirmation, I was terrified by a conception, which, if that were possible, seemed to me even still more daring. The master had been speaking of Golgotha. The Biblical account of the Passion and Death of Christ had, from my earliest years, made a deep impression on me. As a little boy, on such days as Good Friday, after my father had read out to us the story of the Passion, I had lived in imagination and with much emotion in Gethsemane and on Golgotha, in that world so poignantly beautiful, pale and ghostlike, and yet so terribly alive. And when I listened to the Passion according to St. Matthew by Bach, I felt the mystical thrills of this dark, powerful, mysterious world of passion and suffering. I find in this music, even today and in the "actus tragicus," the essence of all poetry and of all artistic expression.

At the conclusion of the lesson Demian said to me contemplatively:

"There's something in this, Sinclair, which I don't like. Read through the story, consider it, there's something there which sounds insipid. I mean this business of the two thieves. It's sublime, the three crosses standing side by side on the hill! But what about this sentimental story of the honest thief, which reads more like a tract? First he was a criminal who had perpetrated crimes, and God knows what, and now he breaks out in tears and is consumed by feelings of contrition and repentance. I ask you what's the sense of such a repentance two steps from the grave? It's nothing but a real parson's story, mawkish and mendacious, larded with emotion, and having a most edifying background. If today you had to choose one of the two thieves as your friend, or if you consider which of the two you would the sooner have trusted, it would most certainly not be this weeping convert. No, it's the other, who's a real fellow with plenty of character. He doesn't care a straw about conversion, which in his case can mean simply nothing more than pretty speeches. He goes his way bravely to the end, without being such a coward as to renounce the devil in the last moment who up to that point has had to help him. He is a character, and in Biblical history people of character always come off second best. Perhaps he's a descendant of Cain. Don't you think so?"

I was dismayed. I had believed myself to be quite familiar with the story of the crucifixion, and now I saw for the first time what little personal judgment I had brought to bear on it, with what little force of imagination and of fantasy I had listened to it and read it. Demian's new ideas, therefore, were quite annoying, threatening to overthrow conceptions, the stability of which I had believed it necessary to maintain. No, one could not deal with anything and everything like that, certainly not with the All Holiest.

As always, he noticed my opposition immediately, even before I had spoken a word.

"I know," said he, in a tone of resignation, "it's the old story. Everything is all right until you're serious

about it! But I'll tell you something: this is one of the
points where one can clearly see the shortcomings of
this religion. The fact is that this God, of the old and
of the new dispensation, may be an excellent conception, but He is not what He really ought to be. He is
everything that is good, noble, fatherly, beautiful, sublime and sentimental certainly! But the world consists
of other things which are simply ascribed to the devil.
All this part of the world, a good half, is suppressed and
hushed up. Just the same as they praise God as the
Father of all life, but pass over the whole sex-life, on
which all life depends, and declare it to be sinful and
the work of the devil! I have nothing to say against
honoring this God Jehovah, nothing at all. But I think
we should reverence everything and look upon the
whole world as sacred, not merely this artificially separated, official half of it! We ought then to worship the
devil as well as God. I should find that quite right. Or
we ought to create a God, who would embody the devil
as well, and before whom we should not have to close
our eyes, when the most natural things in the world take
place."

Contrary to his custom, he had become almost vehement, but he smiled again immediately and pressed me
no further.

But in me these words encountered the riddle of
my whole boyhood, which I had hourly carried with me,
but of which I had never spoken to anyone. What De-

mian had said about God and the devil, about the official godly world and the suppressed devil's world, that was exactly my own idea, my own myth, the idea of the two worlds or two halves of the world—the light and the dark. The realization that my problem was a problem of humanity as a whole, of life and thought in general, suddenly dawned on me, and this recognition inspired me with fear and awe as I suddenly felt to what an extent my own innermost personal life and thought were part of the eternal stream of great ideas. The realization was not joyful, although it confirmed my mode of thought and made me happy to a certain extent. It was hard and tasted raw, because a hint of responsibility lay therein, telling me to put away childish things and to stand alone.

I told my friend—the first time in my life I had revealed so deep a secret—of my conception of the "two worlds," a conception which had been formed since the earliest years of my childhood. He at once saw that I was in thorough agreement with him. But he was not the kind to make the most of this. He listened with greater attention than he had ever given me, and looked me in the eyes until I had to turn away. I again noticed in his look this odd, animal-like timelessness, this inconceivably old age.

"We will talk more about that another time," he said considerately. "I see that you think more than you can express. But if that is so, then you also know that you have never lived in experience all that you have thought, and that is not good. Only the thought that we live through in experience has any value. You knew that your 'world of sanction' was simply one-half of the world, and yet you tried to suppress the other half in you, as do the parsons and teachers. You will not succeed. No one succeeds who has once begun to think."

This impressed me deeply.

"But," I almost shouted, "there *are* horrible things which are really and actually forbidden—you can't deny that fact. And they are forbidden once for all, and so we must renounce them. I know of course that there are such things as murder, and all possible kinds of vice, but shall I then, simply because such things exist, go and become a criminal?"

"We shan't be able to finish our discussion today," said Max, in a milder tone. "You must certainly not commit murder or rape, no. But you haven't yet reached that point where one can see what is 'permitted' and what is really 'taboo.' You have realized only a part of the truth. The remainder will come after, rely on it. For instance, for the past year or so you have had in you an instinct which is stronger than all the others, and which is held to be 'taboo.' The Greeks and many other people, on the contrary, made a sort of divinity out of this instinct, and honored it by great celebrations. What is now 'taboo' is therefore not eternally so, it can change. Today everyone is permitted to

76

sleep with a woman as soon as he has been with her to a parson and has gone through the ceremony of marriage. With other races it is different, even today. For that reason each one of us must find out for himself what is permitted and what is forbidden—forbidden, that is, to himself. You need never do anything that is forbidden and yet be a thorough rascal. And vice versa. It is really merely a question of convenience. Whoever is too lazy to think for himself and to constitute himself his own judge simply conforms to the taboos, whatever they happen to be. He has an easy time of it. Others realize they carry laws in themselves. For them things are forbidden which every man of honor does daily. On the other hand things are permitted them which are otherwise taboo. Everyone must stand up for himself."

Suddenly he seemed to regret having said so much, and broke off. I felt I could understand to a certain extent what his sentiment was. That is to say, however agreeably he used to present his ideas (apparently in a cursory manner) he could on no account tolerate a conversation made simply "for the sake of talking," as he once said. He realized in my case that, although my interest was genuine enough, I was too much inclined to look upon discussion as a game, too fond of clever talking—in short I was lacking in perfect seriousness.

As I read again the words I have just written—"perfect seriousness"—another scene suddenly comes into my mind, the most impressive experience I lived through with Max Demian in those still half-childlike times.

Our confirmation classes were drawing to an end, and the closing lessons were devoted to the Last Supper. The clergyman thought this very important, and he took pains to make us feel something of the inspiration and sacred character of his teaching. However, precisely in those last few lessons, thoughts were diverted to another object, to the person of my friend. Looking forward to my confirmation, which was explained to us as being our solemn admission into the community of the Church, the thought presented itself imperatively to me that the value of this half-year's religious instruction did not lie for me in what I had learned in class, but rather in Demian's presence and influence. It was not into the Church that I was ready to be received, but into something else, into an order of ideas and of personalities which surely existed somewhere or other on earth, and of which I felt my friend was the representative or messenger.

I tried to repress this thought. In spite of everything, I earnestly intended to go through the ceremony of confirmation with a certain dignity, and the new notions I was forming seemed scarcely compatible with this. Yet do what I would, the idea was there, and gradually identified itself with the approaching religious ceremony. I was ready to celebrate it in a different fashion from the other confirmation candidates. For me it would mean admission into a world of ideas, with which I had become acquainted through Demian.

In those days it happened that I had another discussion with him; it was just before a lesson. My friend was wrapped up in himself and took little pleasure in my talk, which was perhaps rather precocious and bombastic.

"We talk too much," he said with unwonted gravity. "Wise speeches have no value at all, absolutely none. You only escape from yourself. To escape from yourself is a sin. You should be able to creep right into yourself, like a tortoise."

We entered the schoolroom immediately after. The lesson began. I took pains to listen, and Demian did not disturb me in my effort. After a while I began to feel something peculiar at my side where his place was, a sort of emptiness or coolness or something like that, as if his seat had suddenly become vacant. The feeling became oppressive and I turned round.

There I saw my friend sitting, upright and in his customary attitude. But he looked quite different from usual. Something I did not know went out from him, enveloped him. I thought his eyes were closed, until I saw he held them open. But they were stiff as if gazing within or directed to an object a great way off. He sat there perfectly motionless; he seemed not to be breathing and his mouth was as if carved out of wood or stone. His face was white, uniformly white, as stone. His brown

79

hair showed more signs of life than did any other fea-
ture. His hands lay before him on the desk, without life,
as still as inanimate objects, like stones or fruit, white
and motionless, yet not relaxed, but as if controlling
the secret springs of a powerful life force.

The sight made me tremble. He is dead, I thought.
I almost said it out loud. But I knew he was not dead.
Mesmerized, I hung on his look; my eyes were riveted
to this white, stone mask. I felt it was the real Demian.
The Demian who was in the habit of walking and talking with me, that was only one side of him, a half. Demian, who from time to time played a part, who accom-
modated himself to circumstances out of mere com-
placence. But the real Demian looked like this, with
just this look of stone, prehistorically old, like an animal, beautiful and cold, dead yet secretly full of fabu-
lous life force. And around him this still emptiness, this
infinite ethereal space, this lonely death!

"Now he has quite retired into himself," I felt with
a shudder. Never had I been so isolated. I had no part
in him, he was unattainable, he was further from me
than if he had been on the most distant isle in the world.

I scarcely understood why no one besides myself
noticed it. I thought that everyone would have to remark him, that everyone would shudder. But no one
gave him any attention. He sat like a picture and, as I
could not prevent myself from thinking, as stiff as a
strange idol. A fly settled on his forehead, moved slowly

down over his nose and lips—not a muscle, not a nerve in his face twitched.

Where, where was he now? What was he thinking, what was he feeling? Was he in heaven or in hell?

It was impossible for me to question him. When I saw him at the end of the lesson living and breathing again, when his glance met mine, was he as he formerly had been? Where did he come from? Where had he been? He seemed tired. His face had its normal color, his hands moved again, but his brown hair was luster-less and fatigued, as it were.

In the days following I practiced a new exercise in my bedroom several times. I sat stiffly on a chair, kept my eyes fixed, and held myself perfectly motionless. I waited to see how long I could maintain this attitude, and what the sensation would be like. However, I merely got very tired, and suffered from a violent twitching of the eyelids.

The confirmation took place soon after, of which no important recollections remain with me.

Everything was now quite changed. Childhood fell about me in ruins. My parents used to look at me with a certain embarrassment. My sisters had become quite strange in their conduct towards me. A disillusionment falsified and weakened the old sentiments and pleasures, the garden was without fragrance, the wood was no longer inviting, the world around me seemed like a clearance-sale of old articles, insipid and without charm, books were merely paper, music a noise. The leaves fall thus from a tree in autumn, the tree feels it not, rain drips on it, sun comes and frost, and the life in it recedes slowly into the narrowest and most inward recess. The tree is not dying. It is waiting.

It was decided that after the holidays I should go to another school, leaving home for the first time. My mother meanwhile approached me with especial tenderness, a sort of preliminary good-by, endeavoring to charm me with a love from which I should go with homesickness and unforgetfulness in my heart. Demian had gone away. I was alone.

Chapter 4

BEATRICE

WITHOUT HAVING SEEN my friend again, I traveled at the end of the holidays to St. ——. Both my parents came with me, and handed me over with all possible care to the protection of a master of the school, in whose house I was to board. They would have been numb with horror, had they only known to what sort of fate they were leaving me.

It still hung in the balance whether I should become with time a good son and a useful citizen, or whether my nature would break out in other directions. My last attempt to be happy under the roof of my father's house and the spirit prevailing there had lasted for a considerable period, and at times had almost succeeded, only in the end to fail completely.

The curious emptiness and isolation which I had begun to feel for the first time in the holidays after my confirmation (how I learned to know it later, this emptiness, this thin atmosphere) did not pass immediately. The parting from home was for me peculiarly easy. I was really rather ashamed of not being sadder—my sisters wept without reason, I could not. I was astonished at myself. I had always been an emotional child, and at bottom, tolerably good. Now I was quite changed. I was completely indifferent towards the outside world. For days together my sole occupation was hearkening to my inner self, listening to the flood of dark, forbidden instincts which roared subterraneously within me. I had grown very quickly in that last half-year, and appeared lanky, thin and immature. The amiability of boyhood had completely disappeared from my character; I realized myself that it was impossible to like me thus, and I by no means loved myself. I had often a great longing for Max Demian; on the other hand, I hated him not seldom, and looked upon him as responsible for the moral impoverishment of my life, to which I resigned myself as to a sort of nasty disease.

In the beginning I was neither liked nor respected in our school boarding house. First they ragged me, then kept out of my way, looking upon me as a rotter and an eccentric character; I was pleased with myself and I even overplayed my part, withdrawing into my solitary self, growling occasional cynicisms. Superficially I appeared to despise the world in most manly fashion, whereas in reality I was secretly consumed by melancholy and despair. In school I could fall back on a knowledge amassed at home. The form I was in was not so advanced as the same form in the school I had just left, and so I acquired the habit of despising my school contemporaries, regarding them as mere children.

This attitude lasted a year and longer. My first holiday visits at home brought no change, I went gladly away again.

It was in the beginning of November. I had formed the habit of taking short, meditative walks in all kinds of weather, during which I often experienced a sort of joy, a joy full of melancholy, contempt of the world and contempt of self. I was sauntering thus one evening through the damp, foggy twilight in a suburb of the town. The broad drive of a public park stood completely deserted, inviting me to enter. The road lay thick with fallen leaves, into which I dug voluptuously with my feet. It smelt damp and bitter; in the distance the trees stood up tall and shadowy, ghostlike in the fog.

At the end of the drive I stood still and undecided, staring into the black foliage, scenting eagerly the damp odor of decomposition and death, which seemed to be in harmony with my own mood. Oh, how insipid life tasted!

A man, with the cape of his raincoat blowing about him, came out of a side path. I was just going on when he called to me.

"Hello, Sinclair!"

It happened to be Alphonse Beck, the senior boy of the house. I was always glad to see him and had nothing against him, except that he always treated me as he did all the younger boys, in an ironical and grandfatherly manner. He passed for being as strong as a bear, was

85

said to have great influence on the house master, and was the hero of many school stories.

"What are you doing here?" he asked affably, in the tone the seniors always used when they condescended on occasion to talk to us. "Composing verse, I bet?"

"Shouldn't dream of it," I disclaimed gruffly.

He laughed, came up to me, and we chatted together in a manner to which I had not been accustomed for some time past.

"You needn't be afraid, Sinclair, that I shouldn't understand. I know the feeling, when one goes for a walk on a foggy evening—the thoughts autumn inspires in one. And one writes poetry about dying nature, of course, and spent youth; which is very much like it. Read Heinrich Heine?"

"I am not so sentimental," I said in self-defense.

"Oh, all right. But in this weather, I think, it does a man good to find a quiet place where one can take a glass of wine or something. Are you coming with me for a bit? I happen to be quite alone. Or wouldn't you care to? I wouldn't like to lead you astray, old man, if you are one of those model boys."

A little while after we sat clinking our thick glasses in a little tavern in the suburbs, drinking wine of a doubtful quality. At first I wasn't much pleased, still it was rather a novelty for me. But unaccustomed to wine, I soon became talkative. It was as if a window had been flung open within me, and the world shining in—for how long, how terribly long, had I not eased my heart by talking. I gave full play to my imagination, and once started, I related the story of Cain and Abel.

Beck listened to me with pleasure—someone at last, to whom I was giving something! He clapped me on the shoulder, told me I was the devil of a good fellow and a clever rascal. How I reveled in communicating my opinions, as I relieved myself of all the pent-up thought of the past months! My heart swelled with pride at finding my talents recognized by someone older than I was. When he called me a clever rascal the effect was like a sweet, strong wine running through me. The world lit up in new colors, thoughts came to me as from a hundred sources, wit and fire blazed up in me. We spoke of masters and schoolfellows, and I thought we understood one another wonderfully well. We talked of Greeks and of pagans, and Beck wished absolutely to draw me out on the subject of women. But on this point I could not converse. I had no experience, nothing to relate. True, all that I had felt and imagined was burning within me, but I could not impart my thoughts, not even under the influence of wine. Beck knew much more about girls, and I listened to his tales with glowing eyes. The things I heard were unbelievable. What I should never have conceived to be possible entered the sphere of commonplace reality and seemed self-evident. Alphonse Beck, who was perhaps eighteen years old, was already a man of experience. Among other things, he told me that girls liked boys to play the gallant with them, but in general were too frightened to go any further. You could hope for more success with women. Women were much cleverer. For instance, there was Mrs. Jaggelt, who sold pencils and copybooks, who was much easier to deal with. All that had happened behind the counter in her shop was unprintable in any book.

I sat on captivated; my head was swimming. To be sure, I could not exactly have loved Mrs. Jaggelt, but still, it was unheard of. It seemed as if things happened, at least to older people, of which I had never dreamed. There was a false ring about it, to be sure, everything seemed more trivial and commonplace, and did not coincide with my own ideas about love, but still, it was reality, it was love and adventure, someone sat next to me who had lived it in experience, to whom it seemed a matter of course.

Our conversation had reached a lower level, had deteriorated. I was no longer a clever little fellow, I was just a mere boy listening to a man. But even then—in comparison with what my life had been for months and months, this was delicious, this was heaven. Besides, as I gradually began to realize, all this was forbidden, absolutely forbidden, everything from sitting in a public house, down to the subject of our conversation. In any case, I thought I was showing spirit; I was in revolt.

I can recollect that night with the greatest clearness. We both of us wended our way home at a late hour under the dimly burning gas lamps through the cool, damp night, and for the first time in my life I was drunk. It was not agreeable, it was in the highest degree unpleasant, but there was a sort of charm about it, a sweetness—it smacked of orgy and revolt, of spirit and life. Beck bravely took me in hand, and although he grumbled at me as being a bloody novice, he half carried, half dragged me home, where, by good fortune, he was able to smuggle us both through a window which stood open on the ground floor.

But a maddening pang accompanied the sobering up as I painfully awoke after a short heavy sleep. I sat up in bed and saw that I was still wearing my shirt. My clothes and shoes lay round about on the floor, smelling of tobacco and vomit. And between headache, nausea and a maddening thirst, a picture came before my mind on which I had not set eyes for many a long day. I saw my home, the house where dwelt my parents. I saw father and mother, my sisters and the garden. I saw my peaceful, homely bedroom, the school and the market-place. Demian and the confirmation class—and all this was bright, lustrous, all was wonderful, godly and pure, all that, I realized now, had until yesterday belonged to me, had waited for me. But now, in this hour, it was mine no longer, it spurned me and looked upon me with disgust. All that was loving and intimate, all that I

89

had received from my parents since the first golden days of my childhood, each kiss mother had given me, each Christmas, each godly bright Sunday morning there at home, each flower in the garden, all that was laid waste, I had trampled on it all with my foot! If the police had come for me then and had bound me and led me away to the gallows as a desecrator and as the scum of humanity, I should have acquiesced; should have gone gladly. I would have found it right and fitting.

That was the state of my feelings. I, who had gone about despising the world! I, who had been so proud in spirit and who had shared Demian's thoughts! So I appeared a filthy pig, to be classed with the scum of the earth, drunk and befouled, disgusting and common, a dissolute beast, carried away by abominable instincts. So I appeared, I who came from those gardens whose bright flowers had been purity and sweet gentleness, I who had loved Bach's music and beautiful poetry! I could still hear, with aversion and disgust, my own laugh, the drunken, uncontrolled, convulsive and silly laugh which escaped me. That was I!

But in spite of everything there was a certain enjoyment in suffering these torments. I had lived for so long a blind, dull existence, for so long had my heart been silent, impoverished and shut up, that even this self-accusation, this self-aversion, this entirely dreadful feeling was welcome. At least it was feeling; flowers were flaring up, emotion was quivering therein. I experienced in the midst of my misery a confused sensation of liberation, of the approach of spring.

However, as far as outward appearances went, I was going fast down the hill. The first debauch was soon followed by others. There was much drinking at school, and other things not in accord with study. I was among the youngest who carried on in this way, but from being just tolerated and looked upon as a mere youngster, I soon rose to be considered as a leader and a star. I was renowned as a daredevil and could drink with the best. Once again I belonged entirely to the dark world, to the devil, and I passed in this world for being a splendid fellow.

But at the same time I was in a pitiful state of mind. I lived in a whirl of self-destroying debauchery, and while I was looked up to by my friends as a leader and the devil of a good fellow, as a cursed witty and spirited drinking companion, my anxious soul was full of apprehension. I remember on one occasion tears started to my eyes when, on coming out of a tavern one Sunday morning, I saw children playing in the street, bright and contented, with freshly combed hair, and in their Sunday clothes. And while I amused and often terrified my friends with monstrous cynicisms, as we sat at dirty tables stained with puddles of beer, in low public houses, I had in my heart a secret, deep reverence for everything at which I scoffed—inwardly I was weeping bitterly at the thought of my past life, of my mother, of God.

There is a good reason for the fact that I was never one with my companions, that I remained lonely even in their midst, that I suffered in the manner above described. I was a hero of drinking bouts, with the roughest of them, I was a scoffer after their own heart. I showed courage and wit in my ideas and in my talks about masters, school, parents, the church—I listened to their smutty stories unflinchingly and even ventured one or two myself—but I was never about when my boon companions went off with girls. I remained behind alone, filled with an ardent desire for love, a hopeless longing, whereas to judge from my conversation I must have been a hardened rake. No one was more vulnerable, no one more chaste than I. And when from time to time I saw young girls pass by in the town, pretty and clean, bright and charming, they seemed to me like wonderful, pure dream women, a thousand times too good and too pure for me. For a long time I could not bring myself to enter Mrs. Jaggelt's stationery shop, because I blushed when I saw her and thought of what Alphonse Beck had told me about her.

The more I realized how different I was from the members of my new set, how isolated I was in their midst, the less easy was it for that very reason to break with them. I do not really know whether the toping and bragging ever caused me much pleasure, and I could never so accustom myself to hard drinking that I did not feel the painful consequences after each bout. I was as if coerced into doing this. I did it because I had to, because I was otherwise absolutely ignorant of a course to follow, I knew not where to begin. I was afraid of being long alone. I was frightened of the many tender, chaste, intimate moods to which I constantly felt myself inclined, I was afraid of the tender notions of love which so often came to me.

One thing I lacked most of all—a friend. There were two or three schoolfellows whom I liked very much. But they belonged to the good set and my vices had for a long time been a secret to no one. They avoided me. With all I passed for a hopeless gamester under whose feet the very earth quaked. The masters knew much about me, severe punishments were several times inflicted on me, my final expulsion from the school was waited for with more or less certainty. I knew that myself; for a long time I had ceased to be a good pupil; I got through my work by hook or by crook, with the feeling that the state of affairs could not last much longer.

There are many ways by which God can make us feel lonely and lead us to a consciousness of ourselves. With me it was in this way: it was like a bad dream, in which I saw myself ostracized, foul and clammy, creeping restlessly and painfully over broken beer glasses, down an abominably unclean road. There are such dreams, when you imagine you have set out to find a beautiful princess, but you stick in stinking back streets full of rubbish and dirty puddles. So it was with me. In this scarcely refined way I was destined to become lonely and to put between myself and my childhood a locked door of Eden over against which stood merciless sentinels on guard in beaming rays of light. It was a beginning, an awakening of that homesickness, that longing to return to my true self.

I was terribly frightened when my father, alarmed by a letter from my house master, appeared for the first time in St. —— and faced me unexpectedly. When he came for the second time, towards the end of that winter, I was hard and indifferent, I let him heap blame on me, I let him beg me to think of my mother, I was unmoved. Finally he grew very angry and said that if I did not turn over a new leaf he would have me disgraced and chased out of the school, and would have me placed in a reformatory. Little I cared! When he went away I felt sorry for him, but he had accomplished nothing; he had found no approach to me, and for a few moments I felt that it served him right.

I was indifferent as to what might become of me. In my peculiar and unlovely manner, with my carrying on and my frequenting of public houses, I was at odds with the world—this was my way of protesting. I was ruining myself thereby, but what of it? Sometimes the case presented itself to me in this wise: If the world had no use for such as me, if there was no better place for us, if there were no higher duties, then people like myself simply went to the devil. So much the worse for the world.

The Christmas holidays of that year were exceedingly unpleasant. My mother was terrified when she saw me again. I had grown taller, and my thin face looked gray and ravaged by dissipation, with flabby features and inflamed rings round the eyes. The first indications of a mustache, and the spectacles which I had but lately taken to wearing, made me look stranger still. My sisters started back and giggled when they saw me. It was all very unpleasant. Unpleasant was the conversation with my father in his study, unpleasant the greeting of a couple of relations, unpleasant above all things was Christmas night. That has been since my birth the great day of our house, the evening of festivity and love, of gratitude, of the renewal of the bond between my parents and myself. This time everything was depressing and embarrassing. As usual my father read the portion of the gospel about the shepherds in the field "keeping watch over their flock by night"; as usual my sisters stood radiantly before the table on which the presents were laid out. But my father's voice was sad, and he looked old and constrained. Mother was unhappy; for me everything was equally painful and unwished for, presents and good wishes, Gospel and Christmas tree.

DEMIAN

The ginger-bread smelt delicious and exhaled thick clouds as of sweet remembrances. The Christmas tree was fragrant and told of things which existed no longer. I longed for the end of the evening and of the holidays.

So passed the whole winter. It was not long before I was severely reprimanded by the faculty and threatened with expulsion. It could not last much longer. Well it made no difference to me.

I had a special grudge against Max Demian, whom I had not seen for the whole of this period. In my first term at St. —— I had written to him twice, but had received no reply; for that reason I had not paid him a visit in the holidays.

In the same park, where I had met Alphonse Beck in the autumn, it chanced that in the first days of spring, just as the thorn hedges were beginning to turn green, a girl attracted my attention. I was out for a walk by myself, full of gnawing cares and thoughts, for my health was bad. Besides that I was in continual financial embarrassment. I owed various sums to my friends and had to invent excuses to procure some money from home. In several shops I had run up accounts for cigars and such things. Not that these cares were very pressing—if the end of my school career was approaching, and if I drowned myself or was sent to a reform school, these trifles would not make much difference either. But I

96

was nevertheless constantly facing these unpleasant things and I suffered from it.

On that spring day in the park I met a girl who had a strong attraction for me. She was tall and slender, elegantly dressed, and had a wise, boyish face. She pleased me at once, she belonged to the type that I loved, and she began to work upon my imagination. She was scarcely older than I, but she was more mature; she was elegant and possessed a good figure, already almost a woman, but with a touch of youthful exuberance in her features, which pleased me exceedingly.

It was never my good fortune to approach a girl with whom I could have fallen in love, neither was it my luck in this case. But the impression was deeper than all the former ones, and the influence of this infatuation on my life was powerful.

Suddenly I had again a picture standing before me, a revered picture—ah, and no need, no impulse was so deep or so strong in me as the desire to revere, to adore. I gave her the name of Beatrice, of whom, without having read Dante, I knew something from an English painting, a reproduction of which I had in my possession. The picture was of an English pre-Raphaelite girlish figure, very long-limbed and slender, with a small, long head and spiritualized hands and features. My beautiful young girl did not completely resemble this, although she had the same slenderness and boyish suppleness of figure, which I loved, and something of the spiritualization of the face, as if her soul lay therein.

I never spoke a single word to Beatrice. Yet at that time she exercised the deepest influence over me. Her picture fastened itself on my mind; in my imagination she opened a sanctuary for me, she caused me to pray in a temple. From one day to another I remained absent from the drinking bouts and the nightly excursions. Once more I could bear being alone, I read gladly, I liked to go for walks again.

I was much scoffed at for my sudden conversion. But I had now something to love and to worship, I had again an ideal, life was once more full of suggestion, of gaily colored secret nuances, that made me insensible to the jeers of my companions. I again felt at home with myself, although I was now the servant and slave of a picture which I revered.

I cannot think of that time without a certain emotion. With earnest striving, I again endeavored to build a "bright world" out of the ruins of that period of my life which had broken up around me, I again lived entirely and single-mindedly in the desire to put away the dark and the bad, and to dwell completely in the light, on my knees before my gods. Still, this "bright world" I built up was to a certain extent my own creation. It was not the action of flying back or crawling back to mother, to a security without responsibilities. It was a new service upon which I entered, invented by myself for my own requirements, with responsibilities and discipline of self. The sex consciousness from which I suffered and before which I was in constant flight was now transmuted in this sacred fire to spirit and devotion. The grim and horrible would disappear, I should groan through no more agonizing nights, there would be no more heart-beatings in front of lewd pictures, no more listening at forbidden doors, no more lasciviousness. Instead of all this, I set up my altar, with the picture of Beatrice, and in dedicating myself to her I dedicated myself to the spirit and to the gods. That part of myself which I withdrew from the powers of darkness I brought as a sacrifice to the powers of light. Not lust was my aim, but purity; not happiness, but beauty and spirituality.

This cult for Beatrice completely changed my life. A precocious cynic but a short while before, I had now become a servant in the temple, whose aim it was to be a saint. I not only renounced the evil life to which I had accustomed myself, but I endeavored to change everything, to set myself a standard of purity, nobility and dignity, which I even applied to eating and drinking, to my manner of speech and dress. I began each morning to wash with cold water, to the use of which I had, in the beginning, to force myself. I behaved with gravity and dignity, carried myself erect and acquired a slower and more dignified gait. To an observer it might have seemed rather ludicrous, but to me it was the performance of a divine worship.

Of all the ways in which I sought to find expression for my new faith, one bore fruit. I began to paint. To start with, the English picture of Beatrice I had in my possession did not bear a sufficient resemblance to Beatrice. I wanted to try to paint her for myself. Full of new pleasure and hope I carried into my room—I had recently been given a room to myself—beautiful paper, colors, and a paint-brush. I made ready my palette, porcelain bowls, glass and pencils. The fine water colors in little tubes which I had bought captivated me. There was a bright chromic green which I think I can see yet as it flashed out for the first time from the little white tube.

I began with caution. To paint a face was difficult; I wished first of all to try something else. I painted ornaments, flowers, and small landscapes from imagination, a tree near a chapel, a Roman bridge with cypresses. I often lost myself completely in this pastime, I was as happy as a child with a box of paints. At last I began to paint Beatrice.

The first few attempts were abortive, and I threw them away. The more I tried to conjure up in my mind the face of the girl, whom I met from time to time in the street, the less I seemed able to transfer my impressions to paper. Finally I gave up the idea, and began simply to paint a face according to the guidance of my imagination, a face which gradually grew out of the one already begun, as if by itself, at the mercy of color and brush. The result was a face I had dreamed of, and I was not ill pleased with it. Yet I made another essay immediately, and each new picture was clearer, and approached more nearly to the type, but was by no means like the reality.

More and more I accustomed myself, in a dreamy sort of way, to draw lines with my brush, to fill in surfaces. My sketches grew out of a few strokes of the brush, out of the unconscious. At last one day I finished a face, almost unconsciously, which made a stronger appeal to me than the former ones. It was not the face of the girl, for I had long since given up the idea of trying to paint my Beatrice to the life. It was something else, something unreal, and yet not of less value for me on that account. It looked more like the head of a youth than of a girl. The hair was not blond like that of my pretty girl, but brown with a tinge of red; the chin was strong and firm, but the mouth was red as a blossom. The features were rigid, like a mask, but impressive and full of secret life.

As I sat before the finished sketch, it made a peculiar impression on me. It seemed to me a sort of picture of a god or of a sacred mask, half man, half woman, ageless, the expression being at once dreamy and strong-willed, stiff and yet secretly alive. This face seemed to have something to say to me, it belonged to me; its look was rather imperative, as if requiring something of me. And there was a certain resemblance to someone or other, to whom I knew not.

The picture played an important rôle for a while, sharing my thoughts and my life. I kept it concealed in a drawer, in order that one should not get possession of it and so be able to sneer at me. But as soon as I found myself alone in my little room I took out the picture and communed with it. Each evening I pinned it on to the wall over against my bed, and gazed at it until I dropped off to sleep. In the morning it was the first object which met my gaze.

Just at that time I began again to dream a great deal, as I had constantly done when a child. It seemed to me that for years I had had no more dreams. Now they came again, quite a new kind of picture, and often and often the painted image appeared therein, living and speaking, friendly or inimical, with the features sometimes twisted into a grimace, sometimes infinitely beautiful, harmonious and noble.

And one morning, as I awoke out of such a dream, I suddenly realized who was the original of the picture, I recognized it. It gazed at me in such a fabulously well-known way, and seemed to be calling my name. It seemed to know me, like a mother, seemed to love me as if since the beginning of time. With beating heart I stared at the paper, at the thick brown hair, at the half-womanly mouth, the strong forehead with the wonderful brightness (it had dried that way of itself) and more and more I felt in me the knowledge, the certainty of having somewhere met the original of the picture.

I sprang out of bed, placed myself in front of the face, and gazed at it from the closest proximity, straight into the wide-open, greenish, staring eyes, the right eye somewhat higher than the other. And all at once this right eye twitched perceptibly, but still decidedly, and from this twitching I recognized the picture. . . .

How was it that I had found it out so late? It was Demian's face. Later I often and often compared the picture with Demian's real features, as they had remained in my memory. They were not quite the same, although there was a resemblance. But it was Demian, nevertheless.

Once, on an evening in early summer the red sun shone obliquely through my window, which looked towards the west. In the room the dusk was gathering. I suddenly had the idea of pinning the picture of Beatrice, or of Demian, to the cross-bar of the window and of gazing at it, while the evening sun was shining through. The whole outline of the face disappeared, but the reddish ringed eyes, the brightness of the forehead and the strong red mouth glowed deeply and wildly from the surface of the paper. I sat opposite it for a long time, even after the light had died away. And by degrees the feeling came to me that this was not Beatrice or Demian but—myself. The picture did not resemble me—it was not meant to, I felt—but there was that in it which seemed to be made up of my life, something of my inner self, of my fate or of my daemon. My friend would look like that, if I ever found another. My mistress would look like that, if ever I had one. My life and death would be like that. It had the ring and rhythm of my fate.

In those weeks I had begun to read a book which made a deeper impression on me than anything I had read before. Even in later years I have seldom chanced upon books which have made such a strong appeal to me, except perhaps those of Nietzsche. It was a volume of Novalis, containing letters and apothegms. There was much that I did not understand. But the book captivated me and occupied my thoughts to an extraordinary degree. One of the aphorisms now occurred to me. I wrote it with a pen under the picture: "Fate and soul are the terms of one conception." That I now understood.

I frequently used to meet the girl I called Beatrice. I felt no emotion on seeing her, but I was often sensible of a harmony of sentiment, which seemed to say: we are connected, or rather, not you and I, but your picture and I; you are a part of my destiny.

My longing for Max Demian was again eager. I had had no news of him for several years. On one occasion only I had met him in the holidays. I see now that I have failed to mention this short meeting in my narrative, and I see that this was owing to shame and self-conceit on my part. I must make up for it now.

So then, once in the holidays, I was parading my somewhat tired, blasé self through the town. As I was sauntering along, swinging my stick and examining the old, unchanged features of the bourgeois Philistines whom I despised, I met my one-time friend. Scarcely had I caught sight of him when I started involuntarily. With lightning rapidity my thoughts were carried back to Frank Kromer. I hoped and prayed Demian had really forgotten the story! It was so disagreeable to be under this obligation to him—simply owing to a silly, childish affair—still, I was under an obligation. . . .

He seemed to be waiting to see whether I would greet him. I did, as calmly as possible under the circumstances, and he gave me his hand. That was indeed his old handshake! So strong, warm and yet cool, so manly!

He looked me attentively in the face and said, "You've grown a lot, Sinclair." He himself seemed quite unchanged, just as old, just as young as ever.

He proposed we should go for a walk, and we talked of secondary matters, not of the past. I remembered that I had written to him several times, without having received an answer. I hoped he had forgotten this as well, those silly, silly letters. He made no mention of them.

At that time there was no Beatrice and no picture, I was still in the period of my dissipation. Outside the town I invited him to come with me into an inn. He came. With much ostentation I ordered a bottle of wine and filled a couple of glasses. I clinked glasses with him, showing him how conversant I was with student drinking customs, and I emptied my first glass at a gulp.

"Do you frequent public houses often?" he asked me.

"Oh yes," I said with a drawl, "what else is there to do? It's certainly more amusing than anything else, after all."

"You think so? Perhaps. It may be so. There's certainly something very pleasing about it—intoxication, bacchanalian orgies! But I find, with most people who frequent public houses, this sense of *abandon* is lost. It seems to me there is something typically Philistine, bourgeois, in the public house habit. Of course, for just one night, with burning torches, to have a proper orgy and drunken revel. But to do the same thing over and over again, drinking one glass after another—that's hardly the real thing. Can you imagine Faust sitting evening after evening drinking at the same table?"

I drank, and looked at him with some enmity.

"Yes, but everyone isn't a Faust," I said curtly.

He looked at me with a somewhat surprised air.

Then he laughed, in his old superior way. "What's the good of quarreling about it? In any case the life of a toper, of a libertine, is, I imagine, more exciting than that of a blameless citizen. And then—I have read it somewhere—the life of a profligate is one of the best preparations for a mystic. There are always such people as Saint Augustine, who become seers. Before, he was a sort of rake and profligate."

I was distrustful and wished by no means to let him take a superior attitude towards me. So I said, with a blasé air: "Well, everyone according to his taste! I haven't the slightest intention of doing that, becoming a seer or anything."

Demian flashed a glance at me from half-closed eyes.

"My dear Sinclair," he said slowly, "it wasn't my intention to hurt your feelings. Besides—neither of us knows to what end you drink. There is that in you, which orders your life for you, and which knows why you are doing it. It is good to realize this; there is someone in us who knows everything, wills everything, does everything better than we do ourselves. But excuse me, I must go home."

We did not linger over our leave-taking. I remained seated, very dejected, and emptied the bottle. I found, when I got up to go, that Demian had already paid for it. That made me more angry still.

This little event recurred to my thoughts, which were full of Demian. And the words he had spoken in the inn came back to my mind, retaining all their old freshness and significance: "It is good to know there is one in us who knows everything!"

I looked at the picture hanging in the window, now

quite dark. The eyes glowed still. It was Demian's look. On it was the look of the one inside me, who knows all.

Oh, how I longed for Demian! I knew nothing of his whereabouts, for me he was unattainable. I knew only that he was supposed to be studying somewhere or other, and that after the conclusion of his school career his mother had left the town.

I called up in my mind all my reminiscences of Max Demian, from the Kromer affair onwards. A great deal he had formerly said came back to me. Today everything still had a meaning, all was of real concern to me! And what he had said at our last, not very agreeable, meeting, about the libertine and the saint, suddenly crossed my mind. Was it not just so with me? Had I not lived in filth and drunkenness, my senses blunted by dissipation, until a new life impulse, the direct contrary of the old, awoke in me, namely the desire for purity, the longing to be saintly?

So I went on, from reminiscence to reminiscence. Night had long since fallen, and outside it was raining. In recollection, as well, I heard it rain; it was the hour under the chestnut trees when he first questioned me concerning Frank Kromer, so guessing my first secrets. One after another these souvenirs came to mind, conversations on the way to school, the confirmation class. And then I recollected my very first meeting with Max Demian. What had we been talking about? I could not for the moment recollect, but I took my time, I thought deeply. At last I remembered. We were standing in front of our house; after he had imparted to me his opinion about Cain. Then he spoke to me about the old, almost obliterated crest which stood over the door, in the keystone which widened as it got higher. He said it interested him and that one ought not to let such things escape one's notice.

That night I dreamt of Demian and of the crest. It changed perpetually, now Demian held it in his hands, now it was small and gray, now very large and multi-colored, but he explained to me that it was always one and the same. But at last he forced me to eat the crest. As I swallowed it, I felt with terror that the bird on the crest was alive inside me, my stomach was swollen and the bird was beginning to consume me. With the fear of death upon me, I commenced to struggle. Then I woke up.

I felt relieved. It was the middle of the night, and I heard the rain blowing into the room. I got up to close the window; and in doing so trod on a bright object which lay on the floor. In the morning I found it was my painting. It was lying there in the wet and had rolled itself up. In order to dry it I stretched it out between two sheets of blotting paper and placed it under a heavy book. When I looked at it the next day it was dry. But it had changed. The red mouth had paled and had become smaller. Now it was exactly Demian's mouth.

I now began to paint a new picture, namely, that of the bird on the crest. I could not recollect any more what it really looked like, neither could I form a clear image of the whole, as, even if one stood directly in front of our door, the crest was scarcely recognizable, it was so old and had several times been painted over. The bird stood or sat on something, perhaps on a flower, or on a basket or nest, or on a tree-top. I did not bother about that, and began with the part I could picture clearly. In answer to a confused prompting, I began straight away with strong colors; on my paper the head of the bird was golden yellow. I continued my work at intervals, when I was in the mood for it, and after a few days the thing was completed.

Now it was a bird of prey, with a sharp, bold hawk's head. The lower half of the body was fixed in a dark terrestrial globe, out of which it was working to escape, as if out of a giant egg. The background was sky-blue. The longer I gazed at the sheet, the more it seemed to me this was the colored crest which I had visualized in my dream.

It would not have been possible for me to have written a letter to Demian, even if I had known where to send it. But I decided, acting under a suggestion which came to me in a dreamy sort of way, as under all my promptings of that period, to send him the picture with the hawk—whether it would reach him or not. I wrote nothing thereon, not even my name. I carefully cut the border, bought a large paper cover and wrote on it my friend's former address. Then I sent it off.

The approach of an examination caused me to work harder than usual in school. The masters had again received me into grace, since I had suddenly changed my vile conduct. I was not, even now, by any means a good pupil, but neither I nor anyone else seemed to remember that, half a year before, my expulsion from the school had been imminent.

My father now wrote to me as formerly, adopting his old cheerful tone, without reproaches or threats. Yet I had no impulse to explain to him or to anyone how the change was brought about. It was merely chance that this change coincided with the wishes of my parents and the masters. It did not bring me into closer contact with the others but isolated me still more. I myself was ignorant of the tendency of the change in me, it might be leading me to Demian, to a distant fate. It had begun with Beatrice, but for some time past I had been living in quite an unreal world with my paintings and my thoughts of Demian, so that she quite disappeared from my mind, as she did from my view. I should not have been able to say a word to anyone of my dreams, of my expectations, of the inner change realized in me, not even if I had wished to do so.

But I had not the faintest desire ever to broach the subject.

Chapter 5

THE BIRD FIGHTS ITS WAY
OUT OF THE EGG

MY PAINTED DREAM-BIRD was on its way, searching out my friend. An answer came to me in the most curious manner.

In my classroom in school I found at my desk, in the interval between two lessons, a piece of paper slipped between the pages of my book. It was folded in the manner we used for passing notes to one another in class. I wondered who could have sent me such a note, as I was not so intimate with any of the boys that one of them should wish to write to me. I thought it was a summons to participate in some school rag or other, in which however I should not have taken part, and I replaced the note unopened in my book. During the lesson it fell by chance into my hands again.

I toyed with the paper, unfolded it without thinking, and discovered a few words written thereon. I threw a glance at the writing, one word riveted my attention. Terrified, I read on, while my heart seemed to become numb with a sense of destiny.

"The bird fights its way out of the egg. The egg is

112

the world. Whoever will be born must destroy a world. The bird flies to God. The name of the god is Abraxas."

I sank into deep meditation after I had read the words through several times. It admitted of no doubt: this was Demian's answer. None could know of the bird, except our two selves. He had received my picture. He had understood and helped me to explain its significance. But where was the connection in all this? And—what worried me above all—what did Abraxas mean? I had never read or heard of the word. "The name of the god is Abraxas!"

The hour passed without my hearing anything of the lesson. The next lesson began, the last of the morning. It was taken by quite a young assistant master, fresh from the University, to whom we had already taken a liking, because he was young and pretended to no false dignity with us.

We were reading Herodotus under Doctor Follen's guidance. This was one of the few school subjects which interested me. But this time my attention wandered. I had mechanically flung open my book, but I did not follow the translation, and remained lost in thought. For the rest, I had already several times had the experience that what Demian had said to me in the confirmation class was right. If you willed a thing strongly enough, it happened. If during the lesson I was deeply immersed in thought, I need not fear that the master would disturb my peace. Certainly, if you were absent-minded or sleepy, then he stood suddenly there; that had already happened to me several times. But if you were really thinking, if you were genuinely sunk in thought, then you were safe. And I had already put to the test what he had said to me about fixing a person with one's eyes. When at school with Demian I had never been successful in this attempt, but now I often realized that you could accomplish much simply by a fixed look and deep thinking.

So I was sitting now, my thoughts far from Herodotus and school. But the master's voice unexpectedly fell on my consciousness like a thunder-crash, so that I started with fright. I listened to his voice, he was standing quite close to me, I thought he had already called me by name. But he did not look at me. I breathed a sigh of relief.

Then I heard his voice again. Loudly the word "Abraxas" fell from his lips.

Continuing his explanation, the beginning of which had escaped me, Doctor Follen said: "We must not imagine the ideas of those sects and mystical corporations of antiquity to be as naïve as they appear from the standpoint of a rationalistic outlook. Antiquity knew absolutely nothing of science, in our sense of the word. On the other hand more attention was paid to truths of a philosophical, mystical nature, which often attained to a very high stage of development. Magic in part arose therefrom, and often led to fraud and crime. But none the less, magic had a noble origin and was inspired by deep thought. So it was with the teaching of Abraxas, which I have just cited as an example. This name is used in connection with Greek charm formulas. Many opinions coincide in thinking it is the name of some demon of magic, such as some savage people worship today. But it appears that Abraxas had a much wider significance. We can imagine the name to be that of a divinity on whom the symbolical task was imposed of uniting the divine and the diabolical."

The learned little man continued his discourse with much seriousness, no one was very attentive, and as the name did not recur, I was soon immersed in my own thoughts again.

"To unite the divine and the diabolical," rang in my ears. Here was a starting-point. I was familiar with that idea from my conversations with Demian in the very last period of our friendship. Demian told me then, we had indeed a God whom we revered, but this God represented part of the world only, the half which was arbitrarily separated from the rest (it was the official, permitted, "bright" world). But one should be able to hold the whole world in honor. One should either have a god who was at the same time a devil, or one should institute devil worship together with worship of God. And now Abraxas was the god, who was at the same time god and devil.

For a long time I zealously sought to follow up the

trail of ideas further, without success. In addition, I rummaged through a whole library to find out more about Abraxas, but in vain. However, it was not my nature to concentrate my energies on a methodical search after knowledge, a search which would reveal truths of a dead, useless, documentary kind.

The figure of Beatrice, which had for a certain time occupied so much of my attention, vanished by degrees from my mind, or rather receded slowly, drawing nearer and nearer to the horizon, becoming paler, more like a shadow, as it retreated. She satisfied my soul no longer. A new spiritual development now began to take place in the dreamy existence I led, this existence in which I was strangely wrapped up in myself. The longing for a full life glowed in me, or rather the longing for love. The sex instinct, which for a time had been merged into my worship of Beatrice, required new pictures and aims. Fulfillment was denied me, and it was more impossible than ever for me to delude myself by expecting anything of the girls who seemed to have the happiness of my comrades in their keeping. I again dreamed vividly, even more by day than by night. Images presented themselves to me, desires in the shape of pictures rose up in my imagination, withdrawing me from the outside world, so that my relations with these pictures, with these dreams and shadows, were more real and more intimate than with my actual surroundings.

A certain dream, or play of fantasy, which occurred to

me, was full of significance. This dream, the most important and the most enduring of my life, was as follows: I returned home—over the front door shone the crest with the yellow bird on the blue ground—my mother came to meet me—but as I entered and wished to embrace her, it was not she, but a shape I had never before seen, tall and powerful, resembling Max Demian and my painting, yet different, and quite womanly in spite of its size. This figure drew me towards it, and held me in a quivering, passionate embrace. Rapture and horror were mixed, the embrace was a sort of divine worship, and yet a crime as well. Too much of the memory of my mother, too much of the memory of Max Demian was contained in the form which embraced me. The embrace seemed repulsive to my sentiment of reverence, yet I felt happy. I often awoke out of this dream with a deep feeling of contentment, often with the fear of death and a tormenting conscience as if I were guilty of a terrible sin.

It was only gradually and unconsciously that I realized the connection between this mental picture and the hint which had come to me from outside concerning the god of whom I was in search. However, this connection became closer and more intimate, and I began to feel that precisely in this dream, this presentiment, I was invoking Abraxas. Rapture and horror, man and woman, the most sacred things and the most abominable interwoven, the darkest guilt with the most tender innocence—such was the dream picture of my love, such also was Abraxas. Love was no longer a dark, animal impulse, as I had felt with considerable anxiety in the beginning. Neither was it a pious spiritualized form of worship any longer, such as I had bestowed upon the picture of Beatrice. It was both—both and yet much more, it was the image of an angel and of Satan, man and woman in one, human being and animal, the highest good and lowest evil. It was my destiny, it seemed that I should experience this in my own life. I longed for it and was afraid of it, I followed it in my dreams and took to flight before it; but it was always there, was always standing over me.

The next spring I was to leave school and go to some university to study, where and what I knew not. A small mustache grew on my lip, I was a grown man, and yet completely hopeless and aimless. Only one thing was firm: the voice in me, the dream picture. I felt it my duty to follow this guidance blindly. But it was difficult, and daily I was on the point of revolting. Perhaps I was mad, I often used to think; perhaps I was not as other men? But I could do everything the others did; with a little pains and industry I could read Plato, I could solve a trigonometrical problem or work out a chemical analysis. Only one thing I could not do: Discover the dark, concealed aim within me and make up my mind, as others did—others, who knew well enough whether they wanted to be professors or judges, doctors or artists. They knew what career to follow and what advantages they would gain by it. But I was not like that. Perhaps I would be like them some day, but how was I to know? Perhaps I should have to seek and seek for years, and would make nothing of myself, would attain no end. Perhaps I should attain an end, but it might be wicked, dangerous, terrible.

I wanted only to try to live in obedience to the promptings which came from my true self. Why was that so very difficult?

I often made the attempt to paint the powerful love-figure of my dream. But I never succeeded. If I had been successful I would have sent the picture to Demian. Where was he? I knew not. I only knew there was a bond of union between us. When should I see him again?

The pleasant tranquillity of those weeks and months of the Beatrice period was long since gone. I thought at that time I had reached a haven and had found peace. But it was ever so—scarcely did I begin to adapt myself to circumstances, scarcely had a dream done me good, when it faded again. In vain to complain! I now lived in a fire of unstilled desires, of tense expectation, which often rendered me completely wild and mad. I frequently saw before me the picture of my dream-mistress with extraordinary clearness, much more clearly than I saw my own hand. I spoke to it, wept over it, cursed it. I called it mother and knelt before it in tears. I called it my beloved and felt its ripe kiss of fulfilled desire. I called it devil and whore, vampire and murderer. It invited me to the tenderest dreams of love and to the most horrible abominations—nothing was too good and precious for it, nothing too bad and vile.

I passed the whole of that winter in a state of inward tumult difficult to describe. I had long been accustomed to loneliness—that did not depress me. I lived with Demian, with the hawk, with my picture of the big dream-figure, which was my fate and my mistress. It sufficed to live in close communion with those things, since they opened up a large and broad perspective, leading to Abraxas. But I was not able to summon up these dreams, these thoughts, at will. I could not invest them in colors, as I pleased. They came of themselves, taking possession of me, governing me and shaping my life.

I was secure in so far as the outside world was concerned. I was afraid of no one. My schoolfellows had learned to recognize that, and observed a secret respect towards me, which often caused me to smile. When I wished I could penetrate most of them with a look, thereby surprising them occasionally. Only, I seldom or never wanted to do this. It was my own self which occupied my attention, always myself. And yet I longed ardently to live a bit of real life, to give something of myself to the world, to enter into contact and battle with it. Sometimes as I wandered through the streets in the evening and could not, through restlessness, return home before midnight, I thought to myself: Now I cannot fail to meet my beloved, I shall overtake her at the next corner, she will call to me from the next window. Sometimes all this seemed to torture me unbearably, and I was quite prepared to take my own life some day.

At that time I found a peculiar refuge—by "chance," as one says. But really such happenings cannot be attributed to chance. When a person is in need of something, and the necessary happens, this is not due to chance but to himself; his own desire leads him compellingly to the object of which he stands in need.

Two or three times during my wanderings through the streets I had heard the strains of an organ coming from a little church in the suburbs, without, however, stopping to listen. The next time I passed by the church I heard it again, and recognized that Bach was being played. I went to the door, which I found to be locked. As the street was practically empty I sat down on a curbstone close to the church, turned up the collar of my coat and listened. It was not a large organ, but a good one nevertheless. Whoever was playing played wonderfully well, almost like a virtuoso, but with a peculiar, highly personal expression of will and perseverance, which seemed to make the music ring out like a prayer. I had the feeling that the man who was playing knew a treasure was shut up in the music and he struggled and tapped and knocked to get at the treasure, as if his life depended on his finding it. In the technical sense I do not understand very much about music, but this form of the soul's expression I have from my child-hood intuitively understood; I feel music is something which I can comprehend without initiation.

The organist next played something modern, it might have been Reger. The church was almost completely dark, only a very narrow beam of light shone through the window nearest to me. I waited until the end, and then walked up and down till the organist came out. He was still a young man, though older than myself, robust and thick-set. He walked quickly, taking power-ful strides, but as if forcing the pace against his will.

Many an evening thereafter I sat before the church, or walked up and down. Once I found the door open, and for half an hour I sat shivering and happy inside, while the organist played in the organ loft by the dim gas light. Of the music he played I heard not only what he himself put into it. There seemed also to be a secret coherence in his repertory, each piece seemed to be the continuation of the one preceding. Everything he played was pious, expressing faith and devotion. But not pious like church-goers and clergymen, but like pilgrims and beggars of the Middle Ages, pious with a reckless surrender to a world-feeling, which was superior to all confessions of faith. He frequently played music by the pre-Bach composers, and old Italian music. And all the pieces said the same thing, all expressed what the musi-

cian had in his soul: longing, a longing to identify oneself with the world and to tear oneself free again, listening to the workings of one's own dark soul, an orgy of
devotion and lively curiosity of the wonderful.

I once secretly followed the organist as he left the
church. He continued his way to the outskirts of the
town and entered a little tavern. I could not resist the
temptation to go in after him. For the first time I had
a clear view of him. He sat at the table in the corner of
the little room, a black felt hat on his head, a measure
of wine before him, and his face was just as I had expected it to be. It was ugly and somewhat uncouth,
with the look of a seeker and of an eccentric, obstinate
and strong-willed, with a soft and childish mouth. The
expression of what was strong and manly lay in the
eyes and forehead; on the lower half of the face sat a
look of gentleness and immaturity, rather effeminate
and showing a lack of self-mastery. The chin indicated a
boyish indecision, as if in contradiction with the eyes
and forehead. I liked the dark brown eyes, full of pride
and hostility.

Silently I took my place opposite him. There was no
one else in the tavern. He glanced at me, as if he wished
to chase me away. Nevertheless I maintained my position, looking at him unflinchingly, until at last he
growled testily: "What the deuce are you staring at me
for? Do you want anything of me?"

"I don't want anything," I said. "You have already given me much."

He wrinkled his forehead.

"Ah, you're a music enthusiast, are you? I think it's disgusting to go mad over music."

I did not let myself be intimidated.

"I have so often listened to your playing, there in the church," I said. "But I don't want to bother you. I thought perhaps I should discover something in you, something special, I don't know exactly what. But please don't mind me. I can listen to you in the church."

"Why, I always lock the door!"

"Just lately you forgot, and I sat inside. Otherwise I stand outside or sit on the curbstone."

"Is that so? Another time you can come inside, it's warmer. You've simply got to knock on the door. But loudly, and not while I'm playing. Now—what did you want to say? But you're quite young, apparently a schoolboy or student. Are you a musician?"

"No. I like music, but only the kind you play, absolute music, where one feels that someone is trying to fathom heaven and hell. I like music so much, I think, because it is not concerned with morals. Everything else is a question of morals, and I am looking for something different. Whatever has been concerned with morals has caused me only suffering. I don't express myself properly. Do you know that there must be a god

124

who is at the same time god and devil? There must have been one. I have heard so."

The organist pushed back his broad hat and shook the dark hair from his forehead. He looked at me penetratingly and bent forward his face towards me over the table.

Softly and tensely he questioned:

"What's the name of the god of whom you are talking?"

"Unfortunately I know practically nothing about him really, only his name. His name's Abraxas."

The musician looked distrustfully around, as if someone might be eavesdropping. Then he bent towards me and said in a whisper: "I thought so. Who are you?"

"I'm a student from the school."

"How do you know about Abraxas?"

"By chance."

He thumped on the table, so that his wine spilled over.

"Chance! Don't talk nonsense, young man! One doesn't know of Abraxas by chance, mark you. I will tell you something more of him. I know a little about him!"

He ceased talking and pushed back his chair. I looked at him expectantly, and he made a grimace.

"Not here! another time. There, take these!"

He dug his hand into the pocket of his overcoat,

which he had not taken off, and pulled out a couple of roasted chestnuts, which he threw to me.

I said nothing. I took and ate them, and was very contented.

"Well," he whispered after a while. "How do you know about—him?"

I did not hesitate to tell him.

"I was lonely and perplexed," I related. "I called to mind a friend of former years who, I think, knows a great deal. I had painted something, a bird coming out of a terrestrial globe. I sent this to him. After a time, when I had begun to lose hope of a reply, a piece of paper fell into my hands. On it was written: 'The bird fights its way out of the egg. The egg is the world. Whoever will be born must destroy a world. The bird flies to God. The name of the god is Abraxas.' "

He answered nothing. We peeled our chestnuts and ate them, and drank our wine.

"Shall we have another drink?" he asked.

"Thanks, no. I don't care much for drinking."

He laughed, somewhat disappointedly.

"As you wish! I am different. I am staying here. You can go now!"

The next time I saw him after the organ recital, he was not very communicative. He conducted me through an old street to an old, stately house and upstairs into a large, somewhat gloomy and untidy room where, besides a piano, there was nothing to indicate that its occupant was a musician. Instead, a huge bookcase and writing table gave the room a somewhat scholarly air.

"What a lot of books you have!" I said appreciatively.

"A part of them belongs to the library of my father, with whom I live. Yes, young man, I live with my father and mother, but I cannot introduce you to them, as I and my acquaintances meet with but scant respect at home. I am a prodigal son, you see. My father is very much looked up to, he is a well-known clergyman and preacher in this town. And I, to let you know at once, am his talented and promising son, who, however, is guilty of many backslidings, and, to a certain extent, mad. I was studying theology, and deserted this worthy faculty shortly before my final examination, although really I am still in the same line, as far as concerns my private studies. For me it is still of the highest importance and interest what sort of gods people have invented for themselves at various times. I am a musician into the bargain, and shall soon get a post as organist, I think. Then I shall be in the church again."

I glanced over the backs of the books and found Greek, Latin, Hebrew titles, as far as I could see by the feeble light of the lamp on the table. My acquaintance, meanwhile, had taken up a position on the floor in the dark by the wall.

"Come here," he called after a while, "we will practice a little philosophy. That means keeping one's mouth shut, lying on one's stomach and thinking."

He struck a match and applied it to the paper and wood in the fireplace, in front of which he was lying. The flame leapt up; he poked and blew the fire with great skill. I lay down near him on the ragged carpet. He stared into the flames, which drew my attention as well, and we lay silent for perhaps a whole hour stretched out in front of the flaring wood fire. We watched it flame and roar, die down and flicker up again, until finally it settled down into a subdued glow.

"Fire worship was not by any means the silliest form of worship invented," he murmured without looking up. Those were the only words spoken. With staring eyes I gazed into the fire. Lulled by the tranquillity of the room, I sank in dreams, seeing shapes in the smoke and pictures in the ashes. Once I started up. My companion had thrown a little bit of resin into the glow. A little slender flame shot up, I saw in it the bird with the gold hawk's head. In the glow which died away in the fireplace, golden glittering threads wove themselves together into a net, letters and pictures, memories of faces, of animals, of plants, of worms and serpents. When I woke from my reveries and looked across at my companion, he was absorbed, staring at the ashes with the fixed gaze of a fanatic, his chin in his hands.

"I must go now," I said softly.

"Well, go then, good-by!"

He did not get up, and as the lamp had gone out, I had to feel my way across the dark room, through dark

128

corridors and down the stairs, and so out of the enchanted old dwelling. Once in the street I stopped and looked up at the house. In not one of the windows was a light burning. A little brass-plate shone in the gleam of the gas-lamp before the door.

"Pistorius, vicar," I read thereon. As I sat in my little room after supper I remembered that I had learnt nothing about Abraxas, or anything else from Pistorius. We had scarcely exchanged ten words. But I was quite contented with the visit I had paid him. And he had promised to play next time an exquisite piece of organ music, a passacaglia by Buxtehude.

Without my having realized it, the organist Pistorius had given me a first lesson, as we lay on the floor in front of the fireplace of his melancholy hermit's room. Staring into the fire had done me good, it had confirmed and set in activity tendencies which I had always had, but had never really followed. Gradually and in part I saw light on the subject.

When quite a child I had from time to time the propensity to watch bizarre forms of nature, not observing them closely, but simply surrendering myself to their peculiar magic, absorbed by the contemplation of their curling shapes. Long dignified tree-roots, colored veins in stone, flecks of oil floating on water, flaws in glass— all things of a similar nature had had great charm for me at that time, above all, water and fire, smoke, clouds, dust, and especially the little circulating colored specks

which I saw when I closed my eyes. In the days following my first visit to Pistorius this began to come back to
me. I noticed that I was indebted solely to staring into
the open fire for a certain strength and pleasure, for
the increase in my depth of feeling which I had felt
since. It was curiously beneficial and enriching—dreaming and staring into the fire!

To the few experiences I had gained on the road to
the attainment of my proper ends in life was added this
new one: The contemplation of such shapes, the surrendering of oneself to these irrational, twisting, odd
forms of nature, engenders in us a feeling of the harmony of our inner being with the will which brought
forth these shapes; we soon feel the temptation to look
upon them as our own creations, as if made by our own
moods; we see the boundary between ourselves and nature waver and vanish; we learn to know the state of
mind by outside impressions, or by inward. In no way
so simply and so easily as by this practice do we discover
to what a great extent we are creators, to what a great
extent our souls have part in the continual creation of
the world. Or rather, it is the same indivisible godhead,
which is active in us and in nature. If the outside world
fell in ruins, one of us would be capable of building it
up again, for mountain and stream, tree and leaf, root
and blossom, all that is shaped by nature lies modeled
in us, comes from the soul, whose essence is eternity, of

whose essence we are ignorant, but which is revealed to us for the most part as love-force and creative power.

Many years later I found this observation confirmed in a book, one of Leonardo da Vinci's, who in one passage remarks how good and deeply moving it is to look at a wall on which many people have spat. He felt the same sensation before those spots on the wet wall as Pistorius and I before the fire.

At our next meeting the organist enlightened me still further on the subject.

"We confine our personality within much too narrow bounds. We count as composing our person only that which distinguishes us as individuals, only that which we recognize as irregular. But we are made up from the entire world stock, each one of us, and just as in our body is displayed the genealogical table of development back to the fish stage and still further, so we have accumulated in our souls all the experiences through which a human soul has ever lived. All the gods and devils which have ever been, whether those of the Greeks or Chinese or Zulus, all are in us, are there as potentialities, as desires, as starting points. If all mankind died out, with the exception of a single moderately gifted child, who had not enjoyed the slightest instruction, so would this child rediscover the whole process of things; it would be able to produce gods, demons, paradises, the commandments and prohibitions, old and new testaments—everything."

"Well and good," I objected; "but then what does the worth of the individual consist of? Why do we continue to strive if everything has already been achieved in us?"

"Stop!" exclaimed Pistorius vehemently. "There is a great difference between whether one merely carries the world in oneself, or whether one is conscious of that as well. A madman can have ideas which remind one of Plato, and a pious little boy in a Moravian boarding school will recreate in his thought profound mythological ideas which occur in the gnostics or in Zoroaster. But he does not realize it! He is a tree or a stone, at best an animal, as long as he does not know it. But, when the first spark of this knowledge glimmers in him he becomes a man. You will not consider all the two-legged creatures who walk out there in the street as human beings, simply because they walk erect and carry their young nine months in the womb? Look how many of them are fish or sheep, worms or leeches, how many are ants or bees. Well, within reach of them are the possibilities of becoming human creatures, but only when they feel this, it is only when, if even in part, they learn to make them conscious, that these potentialities become theirs."

Our conversations were somewhat after this style. They seldom taught me anything completely new, anything absolutely surprising. But all, even the most banal, hit like a light persistent hammer-stroke on the

132

same point in me, all helped in my development, all helped to peel off skins, to break up eggshells, and after each talk I held my head somewhat higher, I was more sure of myself until my yellow bird pushed his beautiful bird-of-prey crest through the ruins of the world-shell.

We frequently related our dreams to one another. Pistorius knew how to interpret them. A curious example comes to my mind. I dreamed I was able to fly. I was flung through the air, so to speak—impelled by a great force over which I had not the mastery. The sensation of this flight was exhilarating, but soon changed to fear as I saw myself snatched up involuntarily to risky heights. There I made the saving discovery that I could control my rise and fall by arresting my breath and by breathing again.

Pistorius interpreted it as follows: "The swing, which sent you up into the air, is the great property of mankind, which everyone possesses. It is the feeling of close relationship with the springs of every force, but it soon causes anxiety. It is cursedly dangerous! For that reason most people willingly renounce flying, preferring to walk according to prescribed laws along the footpath. But not you. You fly higher, as befits an intelligent fellow. And behold, you make a wonderful discovery there, namely, you gradually get the mastery over the impelling force. In other words, you acquire a fine little force of your own, an instrument, a rudder. That is splendid. Without that one goes floating into the air without any will of one's own; madmen, for instance, do that. They have deeper presentiments than the people on the footpath. But they have no key and no rudder, they fall whistling through the air, down into the fathomless depths. But you, Sinclair, you manage all right! And how, pray? You probably don't even know. You manage with a new instrument, with a breath regulator. And now you can see that your soul isn't really 'personal' at bottom. I mean that you didn't invent this regulator. It isn't new. It is a loan, it has existed for thousands of years. It is the balancing organ fish have—the air-bladder. Even today we actually still have a few very rare kinds of fish whose air-bladder is at the same time a sort of lung; and on occasion they can use it to breathe with. In your dream you made use of your lungs in exactly the same way as these fish do their air-bladder."

He even brought me a volume on zoology, and showed me the original drawings of these ancient fish. And with a peculiar thrill I felt an organ of early evolutionary epochs functioning in me.

Chapter 6

JACOB WRESTLES WITH GOD

I CANNOT RELATE in brief all that I learned from the singular musician Pistorius about Abraxas. The most important result of his teaching was that I made a further step forward on the road to self-realization. I was then about eighteen years old. I was a young man rather out of the ordinary, precocious in a hundred things, in a hundred other things backward and helpless. When from time to time I used to compare myself with others, I was often proud and conceited, but just as frequently I felt depressed and humiliated. I had often looked upon myself as a genius, often as half mad. I could not share the pleasures and life of the fellows of my age, and often I heaped reproaches on myself and was consumed with cares, thinking I was hopelessly cut off from them, and that life was closed to me.

Pistorius, himself full-grown and an eccentric, taught me to preserve my courage and my self-esteem. In constantly finding some value in my words, in my dreams, in the play of my imagination and in my ideas, in taking them seriously and discussing them, he set me an example.

135

"You have told me," he said, "that you like music because it is not moral. Well, all right. But you should be no moralist yourself! You should not compare yourself with others. If nature had created you to be a bat, you ought not to want to make yourself into an ostrich. You often consider yourself as singular, you reproach yourself with going ways different from most people. You must get out of that habit. Look in the fire, look at the clouds, and as soon as you have presentiments, and the voices of your soul begin to speak, yield to them and don't first ask what the opinion of your master or your father would be, or whether they would be pleasing to some god or other. One spoils oneself that way. In doing that one treads the common road, becomes a fossil. Sinclair, my dear fellow, the name of our god is Abraxas. He is God and he is Satan; he has the light and the dark world in him. Abraxas has no objection to urge against any of your ideas or against any of your dreams. Never forget that. But he deserts you if you ever become blameless and normal. He deserts you and seeks out another pot in order to cook his ideas therein."

Of all my dreams, that dark love-dream recurred most frequently. Often, often have I dreamed of it; often I stepped under the crest with the bird on it into our house, and wished to draw my mother to me, but instead of her I found I was embracing the tall, manly, half-motherly woman, of whom I was afraid, and yet to whom I was drawn by a most ardent desire. And I could

136

never relate this dream to my friend. I kept it back, although I had opened my heart to him on everything else. It was my secret, my retreat, my refuge.

When I was depressed, I used to beg Pistorius to play me the passacaglia of old Buxtehude. I sat in the dark church in the evening, engrossed in this singularly intimate music, which seemed to be hearkening to itself, as if entirely self-absorbed. Each time it did me good and made me more ready to follow the promptings of my inward self.

Sometimes we stayed awhile in the church after the strains of the organ had died away. We sat and watched the feeble light shine through the high lancet window; the light seemed to lose itself in the body of the church.

"It sounds funny," said Pistorius, "that I once did theology and almost became a parson. But it was only an error in form that I committed. To be a priest, that is my vocation and my aim. Only I was too easily satisfied, and gave myself to the service of Jehovah before ever I knew Abraxas. Ah, every religion is beautiful! Religion is soul. It is all one whether you take communion as a Christian or whether you make a pilgrimage to Mecca."

"Then really you might have been a clergyman," I suggested.

"No, Sinclair, no. I should have had to have lied in that case. Our religion is so practiced, as if it were none. It is carried on as if it were a work of the understanding.

A Catholic I could well be, if need were, but a Protestant clergyman—no! There are two kinds of genuine believers—I know such—who hold gladly to the literal interpretation. I could not say to them that for me Christ was not a mere person, but a hero, a myth, a wonderful shadow-picture, in which mankind sees itself painted on the wall of eternity. And what should I find to say to the other sort, those who go to church to hear wise words, to fulfill a duty, in order to leave nothing undone, etc.? Convert them, you think, perhaps? But that is not at all my idea. The priest does not wish to convert. He only wants to live among the believers, among those of his own kind, so that through him they may find expression for that feeling out of which we make our gods."

He broke off. Then he continued: "Our new faith, for which we have now chosen the name of Abraxas, is beautiful, my friend. It is the best we have. But it is still a nestling. Its wings have not yet grown. Alas, a lonely religion, that is not yet the true one. It must become an affair of many; it must have cult and orgy, feasts and mysteries. . . ."

He was sunk in reflection.

"Can one not celebrate mysteries alone, or in a very small circle?" I asked hesitatingly.

"Yes, one can," he nodded. "I have been celebrating them for a long time past. I have celebrated cults for which I should have been imprisoned for years in a convict station, if they had been found out. But I know it is not the right thing."

He suddenly clapped me on the shoulder, making me jump. "Young friend," he said impressively, "you also have mysteries. I know that you must have dreams of which you make no mention to me. I don't wish to know them. But I tell you: Live them, these dreams, play your destined part, build altars to them! It is not yet the perfect religion, but it is a way. Whether you and I and a few other people will one day renew the world remains to be seen. But we must renew it daily within us, otherwise we are of no account. Think over it! You are eighteen, Sinclair, you don't go with loose women, you must have love-dreams, desires. Perhaps they are such that you are frightened by them! They are the best you have! Believe me! I have lost a great deal by doing violence to these love-dreams when I was your age. One should not do that. When one knows of Abraxas, one should do that no more. We should fear nothing, we should hold nothing forbidden which the soul in us desires."

Frightened, I objected: "But you can't do everything which comes into your mind! You can't murder a man because you can't tolerate him."

He pressed closer to me.

"There are cases where you can. Only, generally it's a mistake. I don't mean that you can simply do everything which comes into your mind. No, but you shouldn't do injury to those ideas in which there is sense, you shouldn't banish them from your mind or moralize about them. Instead of getting oneself crucified or crucifying others, one can solemnly drink wine out of a cup, thinking the while on the mystery of sacrifice. One can, without such actions, treat one's impulses and one's so-called temptations with esteem and love. Then you discover their meaning, and they all have meaning. Next time the idea takes you to do something really mad and sinful, Sinclair, if you would like to murder someone or to do something dreadfully obscene, then think a moment, that it is Abraxas who is indulging in a play of fancy. The man you would like to kill is never really Mr. So-and-So, that is really only a disguise. When we hate a man, we hate in him something which resides in us ourselves. What is not in us does not move us."

Never had Pistorius said anything to me which went home so deeply as this. I could not reply. But what moved me most singularly and most powerfully was that Pistorius in this conversation had struck the same note as Demian, whose words I had carried in my mind for years and years past. They knew nothing of one another, and both said to me the same thing.

"The things we see," said Pistorius softly, "are the same things which are in us. There is no reality except that which we have in ourselves. For that reason most people live so unreally, because they hold the impressions of the outside world for real, and their own world in themselves never enters into their consideration. You can be happy like that. But if once you know of the other, then you no longer have the choice to go the way most people go. Sinclair, the road for most people is easy, ours is hard. Let us go."

A few days later, after I had on two occasions waited for him in vain, I met him late one evening in the street. He came stumbling round a corner, blown along by the cold night wind. He was very drunk. I did not like to call him. He passed by without noticing me, staring in front of him with strange, glowing eyes, as though he were moving in obedience to a dark call from the unknown. I followed him down one street. He drifted along as if drawn by an invisible wire, with the swaying gait of a fanatic, or like a ghost. Sadly I went home, to the unsolved problems of my dreams.

"Thus he renews the world in himself!" I thought, and felt instantly that my thought was base and moral. What did I know of his dreams? Perhaps in his intoxication he was going a surer way than I in my anxiety.

In the intervals between lessons it struck me once or twice that a boy who had never before attracted my notice was hovering about in my proximity. It was a little, weak-looking, slim youngster with reddish-blond thin hair, who had something peculiar in his look and behavior. One evening as I came home he was on the watch for me in the street. He let me pass by, then walked behind me; and remained standing in front of the door of the house.

"Can I do anything for you?" I asked.

"I only want to speak to you," he said timidly. "Be good enough to come a few steps with me."

I followed him, observing that he was deeply excited and full of expectation. His hands trembled.

"Are you a Spiritualist?" he asked quite suddenly.

"No, Knauer," I said, laughing. "Not a bit. How did you get hold of that idea?"

"But you are a Theosophist?"

"No again."

"Oh, please don't be so reserved. I feel with absolute certitude there is something singular about you. It is in your eyes. I thought it certain you communed with spirits. I am not asking out of curiosity, Sinclair, no! I am myself a seeker, you know, and I am so lonely."

"Tell me, then!" I encouraged him. "I know absolutely nothing of ghosts. I live in my dreams: that is what you have felt about me. Other people live in dreams as well, but not in their own, that is the difference."

"Yes, perhaps so," he whispered. "Only it depends on the sort of dreams you live in. Have you ever heard of white magic?"

I had to admit my ignorance.

"It's when you learn to get the mastery over yourself.

You can be immortal, and have magical powers as well. Have you never practiced such experiments?"

On my evincing curiosity with regard to those practices, he was mysteriously silent, but when I turned to go he burst out in explanation.

"For example, when I go to sleep or when I wish to concentrate my thoughts I do such exercises. I think of something or other, a word for instance, or a name, or a geometrical figure. Then I think it into myself, as strongly as I can. I try to get it into my head, until I feel it is there. Then I think it in my neck, and so on, until I am quite full of it. Then my thoughts are concentrated and nothing more can disturb my repose."

I understood to a certain degree what he meant. Yet I felt he had something else in his mind, he was oddly excited and hasty. I tried to make the questions easy for him, and he soon gave me an indication of what immediately concerned him.

"You are also continent?" he asked me anxiously.

"What do you mean by that? Do you mean it from the sex point of view?"

"Yes, yes. I have been continent for two years, since I knew of what I have told you. Before that I practiced a vice, you know what. You have never been with a woman, then?"

"No," I said. "I haven't found the right one."

"But if you should find her, the one you consider the right one, then would you sleep with her?"

"Yes, naturally. If she had nothing against it," I said with some scorn.

"Oh, then you are on a false track! One can only perfect one's inner forces if one remains entirely continent. I have done it, for two whole years. Two years and a little more than a month! It's so hard. Often I can scarcely hold out any longer."

"Listen, Knauer, I don't believe that continency is so terribly important."

"I know," he parried, "they all say that. But I did not expect to hear it from you. Whoever will go the higher spiritual way must remain pure, unconditionally!"

"Well, then, do so! But I don't understand why one man should be purer than another, because he represses his sex instincts. Or can you switch off all sexual matters from your thoughts and dreams?"

He looked despairingly at me.

"No, that's just it. God! and yet it must be. At night I have dreams which I couldn't relate even to myself. Terrible dreams, terrible!"

I recollected what Pistorius had said to me. But however much I felt his words to be right I could not pass them on. I could not give advice which did not result from my own experience, advice the observance of which I did not yet feel myself equal to. I was silent and felt humiliated that someone should come to me for counsel when I had none to give.

"I have tried everything!" wailed Knauer beside me.

"I have done all that a man can do, with cold water, with snow, with gymnastic exercises and running, but all that doesn't help a bit. Each night I wake up out of dreams on which I dare not think. And most dreadful of all, I am by degrees losing everything that I had gained spiritually. It is almost impossible for me any longer to concentrate my thoughts or to lull myself to sleep. Often I lie awake the whole night through. I shall not be able to bear that much longer. Finally, when I can carry on the struggle no further, when I give in and make myself impure again, then I shall be worse than all the others who have never struggled against it. You understand that, don't you?"

I nodded, but could say nothing to the point. He began to bore me, and I was horrified at myself, because his obvious need and despair made no deep impression on me. My only sentiment was: I can't help you.

"Then you know nothing that would help me?" he asked at last, exhausted and sad. "Nothing at all? There must be some way! How do you manage?"

"I cannot tell you anything, Knauer. People can't help one another in this case. No one has helped me, either. You must think of something yourself, and you must obey the prompting which really comes from your own nature. There is nothing else. If you cannot find yourself, you won't find any spirits, either."

Disappointed, and suddenly become dumb, the little fellow looked at me. Then his look suddenly glowed with hate, he made a grimace at me and cried with rage: "Ah, you're a nice sort of saint! You have your vice as well, I know! You pretend to wisdom, and secretly you stick in the same filth as I and all of us! You're swine, swine, like myself. We are all swine!"

I went away and left him standing there. He made two, three steps in my direction, then he stopped, turned round and ran away. I felt sick from a feeling of pity and horror. I could not get rid of the feeling until I got home to my little room, and placing my few pictures before me, I surrendered myself up with passionate fervor to my dreams. My dreams came back at once, the dream of front door and crest, of mother and the strange woman, and I saw the features of the woman so very clearly that I began to draw her picture the same evening.

In a few days this drawing was finished, painted in as if unconsciously in dreamy quarter-of-an-hour periods. In the evening I hung it on the wall, put the reading lamp in front of it, and stood before it as before a spirit with whom I had to fight until victory should be decided one way or the other. It was a face similar to the former, resembling my friend Demian, in certain traits even resembling myself. One eye stood perceptibly higher than the other, the look passed over me, sunk in a staring gaze, full of destiny.

I stood before it. Such was my inward exertion that I became cold to the marrow. I questioned the picture, I abused it, I caressed it, I prayed to it. I called it mother, I called it beloved, called it strumpet and whore, called it Abraxas. Meanwhile words of Pistorius crossed my mind, or of Demian? I could not recollect on what occasion they had been spoken, but I thought I heard them again. They were the words of Jacob wrestling with the angel of God. "I will not let thee go, except thou bless me."

The painted face in the lamplight changed at each appeal. It was bright and shining, was black and gloomy; it closed pale lids over dead eyes, opened them again and flashed a burning look. It was woman, man, girl, was a little child, an animal, vanished to a speck, was again tall and clear. At last, in response to a strong inward prompting, I closed my eyes, and saw the picture inwardly in me, stronger and more powerful. I wished to kneel down before it, but it was so much within me, that I could separate it from myself no more; it seemed as if it had entirely identified itself with me.

Then I heard a loud confused roar as of a spring storm. I trembled in an indescribably new feeling of fear and excitement. Stars darted before me and died out, recollections even of the first forgotten years of my childhood, of a time further back still, of a pre-existence and the early stages of existence, pressed through me. But the recollections which seemed to piece together my life's whole history even to its most secret details did not cease with yesterday and today, they went further, mirrored the future, tearing me away from today, changing me into new forms of life, of which the pictures were very bright and blinding. But of none of them could I call up a just image later.

In the night I woke up out of a deep sleep. I was dressed and lying transversely across the bed. I struck a light, feeling that I must try to remember something important that had happened. I knew nothing of the hours just passed. I turned on the light, and recollection came back gradually. I looked for the picture. It was not hanging on the wall, neither was it lying on the table. I thought confusedly that I must have burned it. Or was it a dream, that I had burned it in my hands and had eaten the ashes?

A great inquietude convulsed me and drove me forth. I put on my hat, went out of the house and down the street, as if under coercion. I walked and walked through streets and squares as if blown along by a storm, I listened in front of the gloomy church of my friend, searched in obedience to a blind impulse, without knowing what I was looking for. I went through a suburb, where brothels stood. Here and there a light was still shining. Further on stood new buildings and brick heaps, covered in part with gray snow. I went on through this wilderness, driven forward by a strange impulse, like a man walking in a dream. The thought of the new building in my native town crossed my mind, that building to which my tormentor Kromer had drawn me to settle accounts with him. In the gray night a similar building stood there in front of me, its black doorway yawning wide. I was drawn towards it, but wanted to shun it and stumbled over sand and rubbish. The impulse was stronger than I, I had to go in.

I staggered over planks and broken bricks into the deserted room. There was a moldy smell of damp, cold stones. A heap of sand lay there, a gray bright speck, otherwise all else was dark.

Suddenly a terrified voice called to me: "In God's name, Sinclair, where have you come from?"

And a human figure rose out of the darkness close to me, a little thin shape like a ghost. I recognized, while yet my hair was standing on end, my school companion Knauer.

"How did you get here?" he asked, as if mad with excitement. "How have you been able to find me?"

I did not understand.

"I wasn't looking for you," I said, dazed. I spoke with difficulty, the words came from me painfully, as if from dead, heavy, frozen lips.

"You weren't looking for me?"

"No. I was drawn here. Did you call me? You must have called. But what are you doing here? It's still night."

He put his thin arms convulsively round me.

149

"Yes, night. But it must soon be morning. Oh, Sinclair, to think that you didn't forget me! Can you ever forgive me?"

"What then?"

"Ah, I was so hateful!"

Then I recollected our conversation. Had that taken place four, five days ago? It seemed to me like a lifetime. But suddenly I knew all. Not only what had occurred between us, but also why I had come and what Knauer wanted to do there.

"You wanted, then, to take your life, Knauer?"

He shuddered through cold and fear.

"Yes, I wanted to. I don't know whether I could have. I wished to wait until the morning came."

I drew him into the open. The first oblique rays of day glimmered indescribably cold through the gray atmosphere.

I led the boy on my arm a little way. I heard my own voice saying: "Now go home, and don't say anything to anybody. You were on a false track, a false track! And we are not swine, as you think. We are men. We make gods, and we wrestle with them, and they bless us."

Silently we went on, and separated. When I came home it was day.

The best that mystery in St. —— had yet to give me was the hours with Pistorius at the organ or by the chimney fire. We read a Greek text about Abraxas together. He read to me portions of a translation of the Veda and

150

taught me to say the sacred "Om." However, it was not this learned instruction which was of service to my inner self, but rather the contrary. What did me good was the self-progression I made, the increasing confidence in my own dreams, thoughts and presentiments, and the consciousness of the power that I carried in me.

I had an excellent understanding with Pistorius in every way. I needed only to think intently of him, and I could be sure that he, or a greeting from him, would come to me. I could ask him, just as I could Demian, something or other, without his being there in person. I needed only to imagine his presence and to put my questions to him as intensive thoughts. Then all the soul-force I had put into the question came back to me as answer. Only it was not the person of Pistorius which I called up in my imagination; nor that of Max Demian, but it was the picture I had painted and of which I had dreamed. It was the half-man, half-woman, dream-picture of my daemon, to which I called. It lived now not only in my dreams, it was no longer painted on paper, but it was in me, as a desire-picture and an enhancement of my spiritual self.

The relation into which the unsuccessful suicide Knauer entered with me was peculiar and sometimes amusing. Since the night I had been sent to him, he dogged my steps like a faithful servant or hound, sought to attach himself to me and followed me blindly. He came to me with curious questions and wishes. He wanted to see spirits, to learn the Cabbala, and he did not believe me when I assured him I understood nothing of all these things. He credited me with being able to do anything. But it was singular that he often came to me with his queer and silly questions just at the moment when I myself had a mental knot to be disentangled. His moody ideas and concerns often gave me the cue, the impulse which helped me in the solution of my own problems. He was often tiresome and I imperiously drove him away. I felt, however, that he had been sent to me, and what I gave to him, I received twofold in return. He also was a guide, or rather a way. The mad books and publications he brought me, and in which he sought the key to happiness, taught me more than I realized at the time.

This Knauer vanished later from my path, neither did I miss him. No arrangement, no understanding was necessary with him. But it was with Pistorius. Towards the close of my school career in St. —— I lived through another peculiar experience with my friend.

Even innocuous, innocent people are not altogether spared the shock of a conflict. Even they come once in their lives in conflict with the beautiful virtues of piety and gratitude. Each must make the step which parts him from his father, from his teachers. Each must once feel something of the bitterness of loneliness, though most people cannot support it for long and soon creep back to their homes again. It was not a great struggle for me to part from my parents and their world, the "bright" world of my beautiful childhood. But slowly and almost imperceptibly I had got further from them and become more of a stranger to them. I regretted it; it often caused me bitter hours during my visits home; but it was not deep. I could bear it.

But when we have offered love and reverence of our own accord, and not out of habit, when we have been disciples and friends with our innermost feelings—then it is a bitter and terrible moment when the realization is suddenly brought home to us that the guiding current of our life is bearing us away from those we love. Then every thought of ours which rejects our friend and teacher enters our own heart like a poisoned sting, every blow of self-defense strikes back into our own face. Then he who felt that the dictates of his own conscience were an authentic guide reproaches himself with the terms "faithlessness" and "ingratitude." Then the terrified heart flees anxiously back to the valleys of childhood virtues, and cannot believe that the rupture must take place, that another bond must be severed.

In the course of time a feeling had slowly developed in me which refused to recognize my friend Pistorius unconditionally as my guide. What I experienced in the most important moments of my youth was my friendship with him, his counsel, his consolation, his proximity. God had spoken to me through him. Through him my dreams returned to me, from his mouth came their explanation, from him I learned their significance. He had given me the courage to realize myself. And now, alas, I felt a growing opposition against him. In his conversation he evinced too clearly a desire to instruct me. I felt it was only one side of my nature that he thoroughly understood.

There was no quarrel, no scene between us, no rupture. I said to him only a single, really harmless word, but nevertheless it was the moment when an illusion between us fell in colored pieces.

The presentiment had for some time already oppressed me, but one Sunday in his scholarly old room this presentiment changed to a definite feeling. We were lying on the floor before the fire. He was speaking of mysteries and religious forms which he was studying, and on which he was meditating. He occupied himself with trying to picture their possible future. To me all this seemed curious and interesting, but scarcely of vital importance. It smacked of erudition. It was like a fatiguing search among the ruins of former worlds. And all at once I felt an aversion from the whole business, from this cult of mythology, from this sort of piecing together, this mosaic work of religious forms which had been handed down to posterity.

"Pistorius," I said suddenly, in a malicious outburst which surprised and frightened even myself, "relate a dream, a real dream, one that you have had in the night.

What you have just been talking about is so—so cursedly antiquarian!"

He had never heard me speak thus. With shame and terror I realized the very same moment that the arrow I had shot at him, and which had entered his heart, was taken from his own quiver—I realized that I had heard him reproach himself in an ironical tone on this very account, and that now I had maliciously turned one of his own reproaches against him like a resharpened arrow.

He felt it instantly, and was silent. I looked at him with terror in my heart and saw that he had become very pale.

After a long, heavy pause he put some wood on the fire and said quietly: "You are quite right, Sinclair. You're a wise fellow. I will spare you all this antiquarian business."

He spoke very quietly, but his tone told me how deeply he had been wounded. What had I done!

I was on the point of tears. I wanted to beg his pardon with all my heart, to assure him of my affection and gratitude. Moving words came into my mind—but I could not utter them. He was silent as well, and so we lay there, while the flames leaped up and then sank, and with each flame that paled fell something beautiful and fervid that ceased to glow and had vanished—never again to come back.

"I fear you have misunderstood me," I said at last, much crushed, and with a dry, hoarse voice. The silly, senseless words came as if mechanically from my lips, as if I had been reading them out of a news sheet.

"I understood you perfectly," said Pistorius softly. "You are quite right." We waited. Then he continued slowly: "So far as one man can be right in his judgment of another."

No, no, a voice inside me said, I am wrong; but I could not say anything. I knew that I had aimed my single little word at his one essential weakness. I had touched the point of which he himself was distrustful. His idea was "antiquarian." He was a seeker, but retrogressive, he was a romantic. And suddenly I realized that it was just what he had been to me and had given me that he could not be and give to himself. He had guided me to a point on the road beyond which he, the guide, could not go.

God knows how I could have uttered such a word! I had not meant it badly. I had had no idea it would lead to a catastrophe. I had uttered something, the import of which I did not myself realize at the moment of utterance. I had surrendered myself to a somewhat witty, somewhat malicious inspiration, and fate used it as her instrument. I had been guilty of a little thoughtlessness, crudeness, and he had accepted it as judgment.

Oh, how much I wished then that he would have got angry, have defended himself, have shouted at me! But he did nothing. I had all that to do within myself. He would have smiled, had he been able. The fact that he could not, showed me more than anything else how hard I had hit him.

And because Pistorius took the blow from me, his presumptuous and ungrateful pupil, so quietly, because he silently agreed with me, because he recognized my word as a judgment of fate, he caused me to hate myself, he made my thoughtlessness seem a thousand times greater than it was. As I struck, I had thought to hit a strong man, capable of defending himself—now he was a meek, suffering creature, defenseless, who surrendered in silence.

We remained a long time lying before the dying fire, in which each glowing figure, each crumbling ash heap called to my memory happy, beautiful, rich hours, making my guilt and my obligation to Pistorius greater and greater. Finally I could bear it no longer. I got up and went. A long time I stood before his door, a long time I listened on the dark staircase, a long time I stood outside in front of the house, waiting to see whether perhaps he would come out to me. Then I went on, walking for hours and hours through town and suburbs, park and wood, until evening fell. At that moment I felt for the first time the mark of Cain on my forehead.

I fell to pondering and rumination. I had every intention, in thinking matters over, to accuse myself and to defend Pistorius. But all ended to the contrary. A

thousand times I was ready to repent of my rash word
and to withdraw it—but it had been true, nevertheless.
Now I succeeded in understanding Pistorius, in building up his whole dream. This dream had been to be a
priest, to proclaim a new religion, to invent new forms
of exultation, of love, of worship, to set up new symbols.
But this was not within his province. He lingered too
long in the past, he knew too much of what had been,
he knew too much of Egypt, of India, of Mithras, of
Abraxas. His love was attached to ideas with which
the world was already familiar. And in his inmost self
he probably recognized that the new religion had to be
different, that it had to spring from fresh sources and
not be drawn out of collections and libraries. His office
was, perhaps, to help men to find themselves, as he had
done with me. But to found a new doctrine, to give
new gods to the world, was not his function in life.

And at this point the realization came upon me that
everyone has an "office," a charge. But to no one is it
permitted to choose his office for himself, and to dis-
charge it as he likes. It was wrong to want new gods, it
was entirely wrong to wish to give the world anything.
A man has absolutely no other duty than this: to seek
himself, to grope his own way forward, no matter
whither it leads. That thought impressed itself deeply
on me; that was the fruit of this new event for me.
Often had I pictured the future. I had dreamed of fill-
ing rôles which might be destined for me, as poet per-

haps or as prophet, as painter, or some such rôle. All that was of no account. I was not here to write, to preach, to paint, neither I nor anyone else was here for that purpose. All that was secondary. The true vocation for everyone was only to attain to self-realization. He might end as poet or as madman, as prophet or as criminal—that was not his affair, that was of no consequence in the long run. His business was to work out his own destiny, not any destiny, but his own, to live for that, entirely and uninterruptedly. Everything else was merely an attempt to shun his fate, to fly back to the ideals of the masses, to adapt himself to circumstances. It was fear of his own inner being. There rose before me this new picture, terrible and sacred, suggested to me a hundred times ere this, perhaps often already expressed, but now for the first time lived. I was a throw from nature's dice box, a projection into the unknown, perhaps into something new, perhaps into the void, and my sole vocation was to let this throw-up from primeval depths work itself out in me, to feel its will in me and to make it mine. That solely!

I had already known what it was to be very lonely. Now I felt I could be lonelier still, and that I could not escape from it.

I made no attempt to reconcile myself with Pistorius. We remained friends, but our relation towards one another had changed. Only one single time did we mention it, or rather, it was only he who spoke of the matter. He said: "I want to be a priest, you know that. I would best of all like to be the priest of the religion of which we have so many presentiments. I can never be that, I know. I have known it already for some time, without fully admitting it. I will do some other priestly service, perhaps at the organ, perhaps in another way. But I must always be surrounded by something which I find beautiful and sacred, organ music and mysteries, symbol and myth, I need that and cannot persuade myself to leave it—that is my weakness. I often realize, Sinclair, that I should not have such desires, that they are a luxury and a weakness. It would be greater, it would be more right, if I placed myself quite simply at the disposition of fate, without pretensions. That is the sole thing I cannot do. Perhaps you will some time be able to do it. It is hard, it is the only thing really hard there is, my friend. I have often dreamed of it, but I cannot do it, I tremble at the thought of it. I cannot stand so completely naked and alone. I am a poor, weak hound, who needs a little warmth and food, who occasionally likes to feel the proximity of his own kind. He whose only desire it is to work out his own destiny has no kith or kin, but stands alone and has only the cold world space around him. Do you know, that is Jesus in the garden of Gethsemane? There have been martyrs who willingly let themselves be nailed to the cross, but even they were not heroes, they were not free, they also wished for something to which they had been accustomed, which they had loved; with which they had felt at home. They had examples or ideals. He who will fulfill his destiny has neither examples nor ideals, he has nothing dear to him, nothing to comfort him. And one really ought to go this way. People like you and me are certainly very lonely, but we still have each other, we have the secret satisfaction of being different, of revolting, of wanting the unusual. But we must drop that, too, if we would go the whole way. We must not wish to be revolutionaries, or examples, or martyrs. To think the thought to its logical end—"

No, one could not think beyond that. But one could dream of it, could sense it, could anticipate it. A few times I realized something of this, in a very quiet hour. Then I looked straight into the open, staring eyes of my fate. They could have been full of wisdom, or full of madness, they could be full of love or full of wickedness, it was all one. One was to choose nothing of all that; one was to want nothing, one was only to want oneself, one's destiny. In that way had Pistorius served me, for a time, as guide.

In those days I walked about as if I were blind, storms roared within me, every step meant danger. I was conscious of nothing but the precipitous darkness in front of me, down to which all the roads I had trodden hitherto seemed to lead. And in my inward self I saw the picture of the guide, who resembled Demian, and in whose eyes stood my fate.

DEMIAN

I wrote on a sheet of paper: "A guide has left me. I stand in complete darkness. I cannot take a step alone. Help me!"

I wished to send that to Demian. Yet I omitted to do this, for each time I wished to do it, it seemed foolish and meaningless. But I knew that little prayer by heart, and often said it to myself. It accompanied me hourly. I began to realize what prayer is.

My school career was over. My father had arranged that during the holidays I was to travel and then I was to go to the University. In which faculty, I knew not. I was to be allowed to take philosophy for one semester. I should have been equally content with anything else.

Chapter 7

MOTHER EVE

IN THE HOLIDAYS I went once to the house in which, years before, Max Demian and his mother had lived. An old lady was walking in the garden. I entered into conversation and learned that the house belonged to her. I enquired after the Demians. She remembered them very well. But she did not know where they were living at that moment. As she felt my interest, she took me into the house, searched through a leather album and showed me a photograph of Demian's mother. I scarcely had any recollections of what she was like. But when I saw the little picture my heart stood still. It was my dream-picture! There it was, the tall, almost masculine woman's figure, resembling her son, with traits of motherliness, traits which denoted severity, and deep passion, beautiful and alluring, beautiful and unapproachable, demon and mother, destiny and mistress. That was she!

I was filled with a wild wonder, when I learned that my dream-picture lived on earth! There was a woman, then, who looked like that, who bore my fate in her features! Where was she? Where? And she was Demian's mother!

163

I started on my travels soon after. A strange journey!
I went restlessly from place to place as impulse directed,
always in search of this woman. There were days when
I met shapes which reminded me of her, and which resembled her. These shapes led me on through the streets
of strange towns, into railway stations, into trains, as in
a tangled dream. There were other days when I saw
how useless my search was. Then I sat inactive, any-
where, in a park or the garden of a hotel, in a waiting
room; I looked into myself and tried to make the picture live in me. But it was now shy and elusive. I could
not sleep, I only nodded for a quarter of an hour or so
on railway journeys through country unknown to me.
Once in Zürich, a woman followed me, a pretty, rather
forward woman. I scarcely noticed her and went on, as
if she were air. I would rather have died at once, than
have shown sympathy for another woman, even if only
for an hour.

I felt that my destiny was leading me on. I felt that
fulfillment was nigh. I was mad with impatience, to
think that I could do nothing to help myself. Once at a
station, I think it was at Innsbruck, I saw, at the window
of a train which was just moving out, a form which reminded me of her, and I was miserable for days. And
suddenly the form appeared again to me at night in a
dream. I woke up with a feeling as of shame, realizing
the fruitlessness and senselessness of my chase, and I
went home by the most direct route.

A couple of weeks later I matriculated in the University of H——. Everything disappointed me. The course of lectures I followed, on the history of philosophy, was just as vain and mechanical as the common ground of student life. Everything was so much according to pattern, one person did as the other, and the boyish faces, although inflamed with a forced gaiety, looked so distressingly vacant. It was like the gloss of a ready-made article! But I was free, I had the whole day to myself, and lived quietly in a beautiful old building outside the town. I had a couple of volumes of Nietzsche on my table. I lived with him, feeling the loneliness of his soul, sensing his destiny, which impelled him onwards unceasingly. I suffered with him, and was happy that there had been one who had gone his way so inflexibly.

Late one evening I wandered through the town; an autumn wind was blowing and I heard the student societies singing in their taverns. Tobacco smoke rose in clouds through the open windows; songs were being roared out, loudly and tensely; but the noise did not soar up, it fell dully on the ear, and was lifelessly uniform.

I stood at a street corner and listened. From two cafés the flood of song rolled forth into the night. Everywhere community, everywhere this huddling together, everywhere this unloading of the burden of destiny, this flight into the warm proximity of the herd!

Two men passed me by slowly. I caught a phrase of their conversation.

"Isn't it just like an assembly of youths in a nigger village?" said one. "They all do the same things. Even tattooing is in fashion. Look, that's the young Europe."

The voice rang suggestively in my ear. I followed behind the two in the dark street. One of them was a Japanese, small and elegant. I saw his yellow smiling face shine under the lamp.

The other spoke again.

"Well, I don't suppose it's any better with you in Japan. People who do not follow the herd are everywhere rare. There are a few here, too."

Every word went through me. I felt pleasure and dread. I recognized the speaker. It was Demian.

In the windy night I followed him and the Japanese through the dark streets, listening to their conversation and enjoying the ring of Demian's voice. It had the old tone, the old, beautiful sureness and tranquillity, and it had the same power over me. Now everything was right. I had found him.

At the end of a street in the suburbs the Japanese took leave and closed a house door behind him. Demian took the way back. I had remained standing, and awaited him in the middle of the street. With beating heart I saw him approaching erect and walking with an elastic step. He wore a brown raincoat and carried a thin stick, hanging from his arm. He advanced with-

out altering his regular stride until he got right up to
me. He took off his hat, displaying his old, bright face
with the determined mouth and the peculiar brightness
on the broad forehead.

"Demian!" I called.

He stretched out his hand to me.

"So it's you, then, Sinclair? I expected you."

"Did you know I was here?"

"I did not know for certain, but I hoped it might be
true. I saw you first this evening. You have been behind
us the whole time."

"You recognized me then at once?"

"Of course. You're very much changed to be sure;
but you have the sign. We used to call it the mark of
Cain, if you recollect. It is our sign. You have always
had it; for that reason I became your friend. But now
it is clearer."

"I did not know. Or rather I did. I once painted a
picture of you, Demian, and was astonished that it was
also like me. Was that the sign?"

"That was it. It's fine that you are here now! My
mother will be glad as well."

I started.

"Your mother? Is she here? She doesn't know me a
bit."

"Oh, she knows of you. She will know, without even
my asking her, who you are. You haven't let me hear
from you for a long time."

"Oh, I often wanted to write, but nothing came of it. For some time past I have felt I should find you. I was waiting for it every day."

He pushed his arm through mine and we went on. Tranquillity seemed to emanate from him and pass on to me. We were soon chatting together as formerly. We mentioned our school-days, the confirmation class and that unlucky meeting of ours in the holidays—only no mention was made of the earliest and closest bond between us, of the affair with Frank Kromer.

Unexpectedly we found ourselves in the middle of a singular and ominous conversation. Having recalled Demian's discourse with the Japanese, we spoke of student life in general and from that we had branched off to something else, which seemed to be rather out of the way of the former trend of our talk. Nevertheless, from Demian's manner of introducing the subject, there seemed to be no lack of coherence in our conversation.

He spoke of the spirit of Europe, and of modern tendencies. Everywhere, he said, reigned a desire to come together, to form herds, but nowhere was freedom or love. All this life in common, from the student clubs and choral societies to the state, was an unnatural, forced phenomenon. The community owed its origin to a sense of fear, of embarrassment, to a desire for flight; inwardly it was rotten and old, and approaching a general break-up.

"Community," Demian said, "is a beautiful thing.

168

But what we see blossoming everywhere is by no means that. It will arise anew from the mutual understanding of individuals, and after a time the world will be re-modeled. What is now called community is merely a formation of herds. Mankind seeks refuge together because men have fear of one another—the masters combine for their own ends, the workmen for theirs, and the intellectuals for theirs! And why are they afraid? One is only afraid when one is not at one with oneself. They are afraid because they have never had the courage to be themselves. A community of men who are afraid of the unknown in themselves! They all feel that the laws of their life no longer hold good, that they are living according to outworn commandments. Neither their religion nor their morals conform to our needs. For a hundred years and more Europe has simply studied and built factories. They know exactly how many grams of powder it takes to kill a man, but they do not know how to pray to God. They have no idea how to amuse themselves, even for an hour. Look at these students drinking in their tavern! Or take any place of amusement where rich people go! Hopeless! My dear Sinclair, no cheerfulness, no serenity can come of all that. These creatures, who move about so uneasily in crowds, are full of fear and full of wickedness, no one trusts the other. They adhere to ideals which have ceased to exist, and they stone everyone who proposes a new one. I feel that there are troubles ahead of us.

They will come, believe me, they will come soon! Of course the world won't be bettered! Whether the workmen kill the manufacturers, or whether the Russians and Germans shoot at one another, it will only be a change of proprietors. But it will not be in vain. It will free the world from the chains of present-day ideals, there will be a clearing away of Stone-Age gods. The world, as it is now, wants to die, it wants to perish, and it will."

"And what will happen to us then?" I asked.

"To us? Oh, perhaps we shall perish as well. They can also murder people in our position. Only we shall not be entirely wiped out. The will of the future will realize itself from what remains of our influence, or with the aid of those of us who survive. The will of humanity will make itself felt, which our Europe has for a long time past tried to drown in its sale yard of scientifically manufactured articles. And then it will be seen that there is nothing in common between the will of humanity and that of our present-day communities, of the states and peoples, of the societies and churches. But what nature wills with man is written in the individual few, in you and in me. It is found in Jesus, in Nietzsche. For these (the only important currents of thought which naturally can alter their course each day) there will be place when the present-day communities break up together."

It was late when we made a halt before a garden by the river.

"We live here," said Demian. "Come and see us soon! We shall expect you."

I cheerfully wended my long way home through the night, which had become cold. Here and there brawling students were lurching through the town. I had often felt, sometimes with a feeling of privation, sometimes with scorn, the contrast between their curious sort of gaiety and my lonely life. But now, tranquil and strong in a sense of secret power, I felt as never before how little that affected me, how far removed was their world from mine. I reminded myself of officials of my native town, worthy old gentlemen, who clung to memories of the semesters they had passed in drinking, as they would to memories of a blissful paradise, and who practiced a cult, calling up reminiscences of the vanished "freedom" of their University life with all the seriousness which some poet or other romantic would devote to an account of his childhood. Everywhere the same! Everywhere they sought "liberty" and "happiness" behind them, in the past, for fear of being reminded of their own responsibility, of being warned they were not striking out for themselves, but merely going the way of all the world. Two or three years passed in drinking and jollification, and then they crept under the common shelter and became serious gentlemen in the service of the state. Yes, it was rotten, our whole system was rotten and these student sillinesses were less stupid and not so bad as a hundred others.

However, when I reached my distant dwelling and went to bed, all these thoughts had flown. Everything else was in suspense as I looked forward to the fulfillment of the promise made to me that day. As soon as I wished, in the morning if I liked, I could see Demian's mother. Let the students hold their drinking bouts and tattoo their faces, let the world be rotten and on the brink of ruin—what had that to do with me? I was waiting for one single thing, that my fate might meet me in a new picture.

I woke up late in the morning from a deep sleep. The day broke for me as a solemn festal day, such as I had not experienced since the Christmas celebrations of my boyhood. I was full of a deep unrest, yet entirely without fear. I felt that an important day had broken for me. I saw and felt the world around me changed: it was full of secret portent, expectant and solemn. Even the gently falling autumn rain was beautiful, full of the quiet, glad, serious music of a festal day. For the first time the outer world was in tune with my inner world—then it is a feast-day for the soul, then living is worth while! No house, no shop window, no face in the street disturbed me. Everything was as it had to be, but did not wear the empty features of every day and of the habitual. It was like expectant nature, standing full of

172

awe to meet its fate. Thus, as a little boy, I used to see the world on the morning of a great feast-day, at Christmas or at Easter. I had not known that this world could still be so beautiful. I had been accustomed to living shut up in myself, and to content myself with the idea that my understanding for the outside world had been lost, that the loss of glistening colors was inevitably connected with the loss of childish vision.

So the hour came when I found again that garden in the suburbs, at the gate of which I had taken leave of Max Demian the night before. Concealed behind trees in a gray mist of rain stood a little house, bright and homely, tall flowers stood behind a big glass partition, and behind shining windows were dark room walls with pictures and bookcases. The front door led immediately into a little hall, and a silent old servant, black, with white apron, showed me in and took my raincoat from me.

She left me alone in the hall. I looked about me. I looked round; and immediately I was in the middle of my dream. On the dark wood wall above a door, under glass and in a black frame, hung a picture I knew well, my bird with the golden yellow hawk's crest, forcing its way out of the sphere. Much moved, I remained standing. My heart felt glad and sorry, as if in that moment everything I had done and had experienced came back to me as answer and fulfillment. Like a lightning flash a crowd of pictures passed through my soul:

173

my home, the house of my father, with the old stone crest over the arch of the door, the boy Demian drawing the crest, myself as a boy, fearsome under the evil spell of my enemy Kromer, myself, as a youth, at the table in my little room at school painting the bird of my dream, the soul caught in a web of its own weaving, and everything, everything up to this moment found echo in me again, and was confined, answered, approved.

With misty eyes I stared at my picture and read in the book of my soul. My glance dropped. In the open door under the picture of the bird stood a tall lady in a dark dress. It was she.

I could not utter a word. The beautiful woman smiled at me in a friendly way beneath features like her son's, timeless and without age, full of an animated will. Her look was fulfillment, her greeting meant homecoming. In silence I stretched out my hands to her. She seized both mine with her strong, warm ones.

"You are Sinclair. I knew you at once. I am very glad to see you!"

Her voice was deep and warm, I drank it in like sweet wine. And now I looked up in her tranquil face, into the black eyes of unfathomable depth. I looked at her fresh, ripe mouth, queenly forehead, which bore the sign.

"How glad I am!" I said to her and kissed her hands. "I believe I have been on my way all my life long—but now I have come home."

She smiled in a motherly way.

"One never comes home," she said gently. "But where friendly roads converge, the whole world looks for an hour like home."

She gave expression to what I myself had felt on my way to her. Her voice and her words were like those of her son, and yet quite different. Everything was more mature, warmer, more assured. But just as Max in years past had made on no one the impression of being a mere boy, so his mother did not look like the mother of a grown-up son, so young and sweet was the breath of her face and hair, so smooth her golden skin, so blossoming her mouth. More queenly still than in my dream she stood before me. Her presence was love's happiness, her look was fulfillment.

This, then, was the new picture, in which my fate displayed itself, no longer severe, no longer isolating, but mature and full of promise. I took no resolutions, I made no vows. I had attained an end, I had reached a point of vantage on the way, from which the further road displayed itself, broad and lovely, leading on to lands of promise, shaded by treetops of happiness near at hand, cooled by gardens of delight. Come what might, I was happy to know of this woman's existence in the world, to drink in her voice, to sense her presence. Whether she would be to me mother, mistress, goddess —what mattered it as long as she was present! As long as my way lay near to hers!

She indicated my picture of the hawk.

"You have never given Max more pleasure than by sending this bird," she said musingly. "And I was pleased as well. We expected you, and when the picture arrived we knew that you were on the way to us. When you were a little boy, Sinclair, my son came one day from school and said: 'There's a boy who has the sign on his forehead, he must be my friend.' That was you. You have not had an easy time of it, but we had confidence in you. Once in the holidays when you were at home, Max met you again. You were at that time about sixteen years old. Max told me—"

I interrupted: "Oh, that he should have told you that. It was the most miserable time I have had!"

"Yes, Max said to me: 'Now Sinclair has the hardest time before him. He is making an attempt to escape to the community, he has even taken to drinking with the others; but he won't succeed in that. His sign has become dulled, but it shines secretly.' Was not that the case?"

"Oh yes, it was, exactly. Then I found Beatrice, and finally a guide came to me. His name was Pistorius. For the first time it was clear to me why my boyhood was so bound up with Max's, why I could not break away from him. Dear lady—dear mother, at that time I often thought I should have to take my life. Is the way so hard for everyone?"

176

She let her fingers stray through my hair, as gently as if a light breeze were blowing.

"It is always hard, to be born. You know, it is not without effort that the bird comes out of the egg. Look back and ask yourself: Was the way then so hard?—only hard? Was it not beautiful as well? Could you have had one more beautiful, more easy?"

I shook my head.

"It was hard," I said, as if in sleep, "it was hard, until the dream came."

She nodded and looked at me penetratingly.

"Yes, one must find one's dream, then the way is easy. But there is no dream which endures for always. Each sets a new one free, to none should one wish to cleave."

I started. Was that already a warning? Was that already a warding-off? But no matter, I was ready to let myself be led by her, and not enquire after the end.

"I do not know," I said, "how long my dream is to last. I wish it would be forever. My fate received me under the picture of the bird, like a mother, and like a mistress. To it I belong and to no one else."

"As long as the dream is your fate, so long must you remain true to it," she said, in earnest confirmation of my remark.

I was very sad, and I wished ardently to die in this hour of enchantment; I felt the tears—for what an interminably long time had I not wept—rise irresistibly and overmaster me. I turned violently away from her. I stepped to the window, and looked out, my eyes blinded with tears, away over the flower-pots.

I heard her voice behind me; it rang out calmly and yet was so full of tenderness, like a cup filled to the brim with wine.

"Sinclair, what a child you are! Of course your fate loves you. One day it will belong to you entirely, just as you dreamt it, if you remain true to it."

I had composed myself and turned my face to her again. She gave me her hand.

"I have a few friends," she said, smiling, "very few, very close friends, who call me Mother Eve. You may call me so as well, if you like."

She led me to the door, opened it and indicated the garden. "You will find Max out there, I think."

I stood under the tall trees, stunned and stupefied. I knew not whether I was more awake or more dreaming than ever. Softly the rain dripped from the branches. I went slowly through the garden, which stretched far along the river bank. At last I found Demian. He stood in an open summerhouse. Naked to the waist, he was doing boxing exercises with a little sack of sand hung from a beam.

Astonished, I remained standing there. Demian looked magnificent; his broad chest, the firm manly head, the uplifted arms were strong and sturdy. The movements came from the hips, the shoulders, the joints of the arm, as easily as if they bubbled out of a spring of strength.

"Demian!" I called. "What are you doing there?"

He laughed gaily.

"I am exercising. I have promised to box with the little Jap; the fellow is as agile as a cat, and naturally just as sly. But he won't be able to manage me. I owe him just one little beating."

He drew on shirt and coat.

"You have already seen mother" he asked.

"Yes, Demian, what a marvelous mother you have! Mother Eve! The name suits her perfectly; she is like the mother of all being."

He gazed for an instant musingly in my face.

"You know her name already? You ought to be proud, young friend. You are the only one to whom she has said it in the first hour's acquaintance."

From this day on I went in and out of the house like a son and a brother, but also like a lover. When I closed the gate behind me, even when I saw the tall trees of the garden emerge in the distance, I was happy. Outside was "reality," outside were streets and houses, human beings and institutions, libraries and lecture rooms— here inside were love and the life of the soul, here was the kingdom of fairy stories and dreams. And yet we lived by no means shut off from the world. In thought and word we often lived in its midst, only on another plane. We were not separated from the majority of creatures by boundaries, but rather by a different sort of vision. Our task was to be, as it were, an island in the world, perhaps an example, in any case to proclaim that it was possible to live a different sort of life. I, who had been isolated for so long, learned to what extent community of feeling is possible between people who have experienced complete loneliness. I no longer desired to be back at the tables of the happy, at the feasts of the merry. I no longer felt envious or homesick when I saw others living in community. And slowly I was initiated into the mystery of those who bore "the sign."

We, who bore the sign, were probably justly considered by the world as peculiar—yes, mad even, and dangerous. For we were awake, or were waking, and our endeavor was to be more and more completely awake, whereas the others strove to be happy, attaching themselves to the herd, the opinions and ideals of which they made their own, taking up the same duties, making their life and happiness depend on common interests. True, there was a certain greatness, a vigorousness, in their endeavor. But whereas, from our point of view, we who bore the sign carried out the will of nature as individuals and as men of the future, the others persisted in a stubbornness which hindered all progress. For them mankind, which they loved just as we did— was something already complete, which must be maintained and protected. For us mankind was a distant future, to which we were all on the way. No one could image this future, neither did its laws stand written in any book.

Besides Mother Eve, Max and myself, there belonged to our circle in a greater or lesser degree of intimacy many seekers of very various sorts. Many of them were going along their own special paths, had set up special aims and adhered to special opinions and duties. Amongst these were astrologers and cabbalists, also an adherent of Count Tolstoy, and all kinds of tender, timid, sensitive people, followers of new sects, men who practiced Indian cults, vegetarians and others. With all these we had really nothing of a spiritual nature in common, except the esteem which each accorded the secret life-dream of the other. Some were in closer contact with us, such as those who traced the searchings of mankind after gods and new ideals in the past, and whose studies often reminded me of my friend Pistorius. They brought books with them, translated for us texts from ancient tongues and showed us illustrations of ancient symbols and rites. They taught us to see how all the ideals of mankind up to the present have their origin in dreams of the subconscious soul, dreams in which humanity is, as it were, feeling its way forward into the future, guided by premonitions of the future's potentialities. So we went through the religious history of the ancient world with its thousand gods, to the dawn of Christianity. The confessions of the isolated saints were known to us, and the changes of religion from race to

race. And from all the knowledge we thus acquired re-
sulted a criticism of our era and of present-day Europe,
of this continent which through enormous exertions
had created powerful new weapons for humanity, only
to fall finally into a deep spiritual devastation, the effects
of which were at last being felt. For it had gained the
whole world, only to lose its own soul.

There were with us believers as well, advocates of
doctrines of salvation, in the efficacy of which they were
very hopeful. There were Buddhists who wished to convert Europe, and disciples of Tolstoy, and of other confessions. We in our narrow circle listened, but accepted
none of these doctrines except as symbols. We who bore
the sign had no cares as regarded the formation of the
future. To us every confession, every doctrine of salvation appeared in advance dead and useless. Our whole
duty, our destiny, was, we felt, to attain to self-realization, in order that in us nature might find scope for its
full activities, and that the unknown future might find
us ready to fill any rôle which should be allotted us.

Whether we expressed our opinion in so many words
or not, it was clear to all of us that a break-up of the
present-day world was approaching, to be followed by a
new birth. Demian said to me on more than one occasion: "What will come is beyond conception. The soul
of Europe is an animal which has been chained up for
an immeasurably long period. When it is set free, its
first movements will not display much amiability. But

the way it will take, whether direct or indirect, is not of importance, provided that the soul's true need is realized, this soul which has been deluded and dulled for so long. Then our day will come, then we shall be needed, not as guides or new law-givers—we shall not live to see the new laws—but rather as volunteers, as those who are ready to follow and to stand wherever fate shall call us. Look, all men are ready to perform the incredible, when their ideals are threatened. But no one comes forward when a new ideal, a new, perhaps dangerous and uncanny impulse of spiritual growth declares itself. We shall be of those few who are there, ready to go forward. For that purpose have we been signaled out just as Cain was marked with the sign to inspire fear and hate, to drive the men of his time out of a narrow idyllic existence into the broad pastures of a greater destiny. All men whose influence has affected the march of humanity, all such, without differentiation, owe their capabilities and their efficacy to the fact that they were ready to do the bidding of destiny. That applies to Napoleon and Bismarck. The immediate purpose to which they direct their energies does not lie within their choice. If Bismarck had understood the social democrats and had thrown in his lot with them, he would have been a prudent fellow, but he would never have been the instrument of fate. The same applies to Napoleon, to Caesar, to Loyola, to all of them! One must always look at such things from the point of view of biology and evolution! When the changes which took place in the earth's surface transferred to the land animals which lived in water, and vice versa, then those specimens which were ready to fulfill their functions as instruments of fate, brought new and unheard-of things to pass and were able, through new adaptations, to save their kind. Whether these specimens were the same that had previously been conservatives and preservers of the status quo or the eccentrics and revolutionaries, is not known. They were ready to be used by fate, and for that reason were able to help their race through a new stage of evolution. That we do know. For that reason we want to be ready."

Mother Eve was often present when such conversations took place, but she did not join in. For each of us who chose to express his thoughts she was as it were a listener and an echo, full of confidence, full of understanding. It appeared as if our ideas all emanated from her and returned to her again. My happiness consisted in sitting near her, in hearing her voice from time to time, and in participating in that atmosphere of maturity and of the soul, which surrounded her.

She felt immediately when a change was taking place in me, when my soul was troubled, or when a renewal was in progress. It seemed to me as if the dreams I had in my sleep were inspired by her. I often related them to her. She found them quite comprehensible and natural, there were no peculiarities which she could not follow clearly. For a time I had dreams which were like reproductions of the day's conversation. I dreamed that the whole world was in revolt, and that I, alone or with Demian, tensely waited the signal of fate. Fate remained half concealed, but bore somehow or other the traits of Mother Eve—to be chosen or rejected by her, that was fate.

Sometimes she said with a smile: "Your dream is not complete, Sinclair, you have forgotten the best part"— and it sometimes happened that I recalled it then, and I could not understand how I had come to forget any of it.

At times I was discontented and was tormented by desire, I thought I could not bear to see her near me any longer without taking her in my arms. She noticed that immediately. Once, when I had stayed away for several days and had returned distraught, she took me aside and said: "You should not give yourself up to wishes in which you do not believe, I know what you wish. You must give up these desires, or else surrender yourself to them completely. If one day you are able to ask, convinced that your wishes will be fulfilled, then you will find satisfaction. But you wish, and repent again, and are afraid. You must overcome all that. I will tell you a fairy-tale."

And she told me of a youth who was in love with a star. He stood on the sea-shore, stretched out his hands, and prayed to the star. He dreamed of it and all his thoughts were of it. But he knew, or thought he knew, that a star could not be embraced by a man. He held it to be his fate to love a star without hope of fulfillment, and he created from this thought a whole life-poem about renunciation, and mute, faithful suffering which should better him and purify him. But his dreams all went up to the star. Once again he stood at night by the sea-shore, on a high cliff. He gazed at the star, and his love for it flamed up within him. And in a moment of great longing he made a spring, throwing himself into space to meet the star. But at the moment of leaping, the thought flashed through his mind: it is impossible! And so he was dashed to pieces on the rocks below. He did not know how to love. Had he had the strength of soul, at the moment of leaping, to believe in the fulfillment of his wish, he would have flown up and have been united with the star.

"Love must not beg," she said, "nor demand either. Love must have the force to be absolutely certain of itself. Then it is attracted no longer, but attracts. Sinclair, I am attracting your love. As soon as you attract my love, I shall come. I do not want to make a present of myself. I want to be won."

On a later occasion she told me another fairy story. There was a lover, who loved without hope of success. He withdrew entirely into himself and thought his love would consume him. The world was lost to him, he saw the blue sky and the green wood no longer, he did not hear the murmuring of the stream, or the notes of the harp; all that meant nothing to him, and he became poor and miserable. But his love grew, and he would much rather have died and have made an end of it all than renounce the chance of possessing the beautiful woman whom he loved. Then he suddenly felt that his love had consumed everything else in him, it became powerful and exercised an irresistible attraction, the beautiful woman had to follow, she came and he stood with outstretched arms to draw her to him. But as she stood before him, she was completely transformed, and with a thrill he felt and saw that he had drawn into his embrace the whole world, which he had lost. She stood before him and surrendered herself to him, sky and wood and brook, all was decked out in lovely new colors, all belonged to him, and spoke his tongue. And instead of merely winning a woman, he had taken the whole world to his heart, and each star in the heaven glowed in him, and twinkling, communicated desire to his soul. He had loved, and thereby had found himself. But most people love only to lose themselves thereby.

My whole life seemed to be contained in my love for Mother Eve. But every day she looked different. Many times I felt decidedly that it was not her person for which my whole being was striving, but that she was a symbol of my inward self, and that she wished only to lead me to see more deeply into myself. I often heard words fall from her lips, which sounded like answers to the burning questions asked by my sub-conscious self. Then again there were moments when in her presence I burnt with desire, and afterwards kissed objects she had touched. And by degrees sensual and unsensual love, reality and symbol merged into one another. Then it happened that I could think of her at home in my room with quiet fervor. I thought I felt her hand in mine and my lips pressed to hers. Or I was at her house, gazing up into her face, talking with her and listening to her voice; and I did not know whether it was really she, or whether it was a dream. I began to foresee how one can have a lasting and immortal love. In reading a book I had acquired new knowledge, and it was the same feeling as a kiss from Mother Eve. She stroked my hair and smiled at me, I sensed the perfume of her warm ripe mouth, and I had the same feeling as if I had been making progress within myself. All that was important and fateful for me seemed to be contained in her. She could transform herself into each of my thoughts, and every one of my thoughts was transformed into her.

I feared that it would be torture to spend the two weeks of the Christmas holidays, separated from Mother Eve, with my parents at home. But it was no torture, it was lovely to be at home and to think of her. When I returned to H—— I remained away from her house another two days, in order to enjoy the security and independence of her actual presence. I also had dreams in which my union with her was accomplished by way of allegory. She was a sea, into which I, a river, flowed. She was a star, and I myself was a star on my way to her. We felt drawn to one another. We met, and remained together always, turning blissfully round one another in close-lying orbits, to the music of the spheres.

I related this dream to her, when I visited her again after the holidays.

"It is a beautiful dream," she said softly. "See that it comes true!"

There came a day in early spring that I shall never forget. I entered the hall. A window stood open and the heavy scent of hyacinths, wafted by a warm breath of air, permeated the room. As no one was to be seen, I went upstairs to Max Demian's study. I knocked softly on the door and entered without waiting for permission, as I was in the habit of doing with him.

The room was dark. The curtains were all drawn. The door to a little room adjoining stood open, where Max had set up a chemical laboratory. From there came the bright, white light of the spring sun, shining through rain clouds. I thought no one was there and pulled back one of the curtains.

There I saw Max Demian, sitting on a stool by a curtained window. His attitude was cramped and he was oddly changed. The thought flashed through me: You have seen him like this once before! His arms were motionless at his side, his hands in his lap; his face in-

clined slightly forward, with open eyes, was without
sight, as if dead. In the eyes there glimmered dully a
little reflex of light, as in a piece of glass. The pale face
was self-absorbed and without any expression, save that
of great rigidity. He looked like a very ancient mask of
an animal at the door of a temple. He appeared not to
be breathing.

The recollection came to me—thus, exactly thus, had
I once seen him, many years ago, when I was still quite
a boy. Thus had his eyes stared inwards, thus his hands
had been lying motionless, close to one another, a fly
had been crawling over his face. And he had then, six
years ago perhaps, looked just as old and as ageless, not
a wrinkle in his face had changed.

I was frightened, and went softly out of the room and
down the stairs. In the hall I met Mother Eve. She was
pale and seemed tired: I had not seen her like that before. A shadow came through the window, the bright
white sun had suddenly disappeared.

"I went into Max's room," I whispered hastily. "Has
anything happened? He is asleep, or absorbed, I don't
know what; I once saw him like that before."

"But you didn't wake him?" she asked quickly.

"No. He did not hear me. I came out immediately.
Mother Eve, tell me, what is the matter with him?"

She passed her hand over her forehead.

"Don't worry, Sinclair, nothing has happened to him.
He has retired into himself. It will not last long."

She got up and went out into the garden, although it had begun to rain. I felt that I must not follow her. So I walked up and down in the hall, inhaling the scent of the hyacinths which dulled my senses, and gazing at my picture of the bird over the door. I felt oppressively the odd shadow which seemed to fill the house that morning. What was it? What had happened?

Mother Eve came back soon. Raindrops hung in her dark hair. She sat down in her easy chair. She was very tired. I went to her, bent down and kissed the raindrops in her hair. Her eyes were bright and soft, but the raindrops tasted like tears.

"Shall I go and see how he is?" I asked in a whisper.

She smiled weakly.

"Don't be a child, Sinclair!" she admonished loudly, as if to relieve her own feelings. "Go now and come back later, I cannot talk to you now."

I went. I walked out of the house and out of the town, towards the mountains. The thin rain was falling obliquely, and clouds were driving at a low altitude under heavy pressure, as if in fear. Down below there was hardly any breeze, but on the heights above a storm seemed to be raging. Several times the sun, pale and bright, broke for an instant through the steely gray of the clouds.

There came a fleecy, yellow cloud driving across the sky. It collided with the gray cloud wall, and in a few seconds the wind formed a picture of the yellow and blue, of a bird of giant size, which tore itself free from the blue mêlée and with wide fluttering wings disappeared in the sky. Then the storm became audible and rain mixed with hail rattled down. A short burst of thunder with an unnatural and terrific sound cracked over the whipped landscape. Immediately after the sun broke through and on the mountains close at hand above brown woods glistened, pale and unreal, the fresh snow.

When I returned after several hours, wet from the rain and wind, Demian himself opened the front door to me.

He took me with him up to his room. A gas flame burned in the laboratory, paper lay about, he appeared to have been working.

"Sit down," he invited, "you must be tired, it was a terrible storm; it's evident, you were overtaken by it. Tea is coming at once."

"Something is the matter today," I began hesitatingly, "it can't only be that bit of a storm."

He looked at me penetratingly.

"Have you seen anything?"

"Yes. I saw a picture clearly in the clouds, for an instant."

"What sort of a picture?"

"It was a bird."

"The hawk? Was it that? The bird of your dream?"

"Yes, it was my hawk. It was yellow and of giant size, it flew up into the blue-black heaven."

Demian took a deep breath. Someone knocked at the door. The aged servant brought in tea.

"Take a cup, Sinclair, do. I don't think it was by chance you saw the bird."

"Chance? Does one see such things by chance?"

"Well, no. It means something. Do you know what?"

"No. I only feel, it means a violent shock, the approach of fate. I think it will affect all of us."

He walked violently up and down.

"The approach of fate!" he exclaimed loudly. "I dreamed the same thing myself last night, and my mother yesterday had a premonition, portending the same thing. I dreamed I was going up a ladder, placed against a tree trunk or a tower. When I reached the top I saw the whole country. It was a wide plain, with towns and villages burning. I cannot yet relate everything, because it isn't all quite clear to me."

"Do you interpret the dream as affecting you?" I asked.

"Me? Naturally. No one dreams of what does not concern him. But it does not concern me alone, you are right. I distinguish tolerably well between the dreams which indicate agitation of my own soul, and the others, the rare ones, which bear on the fate of all humanity. I have seldom had such dreams, and never one of which I

can say that it was a prophecy, and that it has been fulfilled. The interpretations are too uncertain. But this I
know for a certainty, I have dreamed of something which
does not concern me alone. For the dream belongs to
others, former ones I have had; this is the continuation.
These are the dreams, Sinclair, in which I had the premonitions which I have already mentioned to you. We
know that the world is absolutely rotten, but that is no
reason to prophesy its ruin, or to make a prophecy of a
like nature. But for several years past I have had dreams,
from which I conclude, or feel, or what you will, which,
then, give me the feeling that the break-up of an old
world is drawing near. At first they were simply faint
presentiments, but since they have become more and
more significant. Even now I know nothing more than
that something big and terrible is approaching, which
will concern me. Sinclair, we shall go through the experiences of which we have so often talked. The world
is about to renew itself. It smacks of death. Nothing
new comes without death. It is more terrible than I had
thought."

Frightened, I looked at him fixedly.

"Can't you tell me the rest of your dream?" I begged
timidly.

He shook his head.

"No."

The door opened and Mother Eve entered.

"There you are, sitting together! Children, I hope you aren't sad?"

She looked fresh, her fatigue had quite vanished. Demian smiled at her, she came to us as a mother comes to frightened children.

"We aren't sad, mother. We were simply trying to solve the riddle of these new signs. But that is of no importance; what is to come, will be here all of a sudden, and then we shall learn what we need to know."

But I did not feel happy. When I said good-by and went down alone through the hall, I felt that the hyacinths were faded and withered, reminding me of corpses. A shadow had fallen over us.

Chapter 8

BEGINNING OF THE END

It HAD BEEN DECIDED that I should remain in H—— for the summer semester. Instead of staying in the house, we were almost always in the garden by the river. The Japanese, who by the way had been thoroughly beaten in the boxing match, was away, and the disciple of Tolstoy was also missing. Demian had procured a horse, and went for long rides every day. I was often alone with his mother.

Sometimes I wondered greatly at the peaceableness of my life. I had been so long accustomed to being alone, to practice renunciation, to fight toilfully my own battles, that these months in H—— seemed to me like a time passed on a dream island, where I might live tranquilly in beautiful, enchanted surroundings. I felt that this was a foretaste of that new, higher community, on which we meditated. And now and then I was seized by a deep feeling of sadness, for I knew that this happiness could not last. I was not destined to breathe in the fullness of peace and comfort, I needed torment to spur me on. I felt that one day I should wake up from these dreams of beautiful love-pictures to find myself standing once more alone, in the cold world of others, where for me there would be only loneliness and fighting, no peace, no community of spirit.

Then I yielded myself to the charms of Mother Eve's presence. My feeling for her was now doubly tender. I was glad that my fate bore still these beautiful, tranquil features.

The summer weeks passed quickly and easily. Already the semester was drawing to a close. Leave-taking was near, I dared not think of it, and did not, but clung to the beautiful days like a butterfly to a honeyed flower. That was my period of happiness, the first fulfillment of my life's wishes, and my reception into the league—what was to come next? I would again have to fight my battles, be consumed by longing, have dreams, be alone.

At this time the feeling, the foretaste of separation, came over me so strongly that my love for Mother Eve blazed up suddenly, causing me pain. My God! how soon would the time come to say good-by, and I should see her no more, no more hear her firm step in the house, should find no more her flowers on my table! And what had I attained? I had dreamed and had lulled myself in comfort, instead of winning her, instead of fighting for her and drawing her to me for always! All that she had said to me about genuine love crossed my mind, hundreds of fine, suggestive words, a hundred tender invitations, promises perhaps—and what had I made of them? Nothing! Nothing!

I took up a position in the middle of my room, collected my whole conscious self together and thought of Eve. I wished to concentrate the forces of my soul, in order to let her feel my love, in order to draw her to me. She was to come, longing for my embrace. My kisses were to suck insatiably the ripe fruit of her lips.

I stood tense, until fingers and feet became stiff with cold. I felt force was going out of me. For a few seconds something seemed to take shape with me, something bright and cool; I had for a moment the sensation as if I carried a crystal in my heart, and I knew that was myself. A cold chill pierced to my heart.

As I woke out of my fearful state of tension I felt something was approaching. I was exhausted to the point of death, but I was prepared to see Eve step into the room, burning with passion, ravished.

The sound of horse's hoofs clattering down the long street rang nearer and nearer, then suddenly ceased. I sprang to the window. Below Demian was dismounting.

"What is the matter, Demian? Nothing can have happened to your mother?"

He did not listen to my words. He was very pale, and perspiration ran down both sides of his forehead over his cheeks. His horse was flecked with foam. He tied the reins to the garden fence, then he took my arm and walked with me down the street.

"Have you already heard the news?" I had heard nothing.

Demian pressed my arm and turned his face to me, with a dark, compassionate, singular look.

"Yes, old man, now we're in for it. You know of the strained relations with Russia—"

"What? Is it war? I had never believed it."

He spoke in an undertone, although no one was near.

"It is not yet declared. But it's war. Rely on it. I haven't worried you lately, but I have seen three new omens since. It will be no foundering of the world, no earthquake, no revolution. It's war. You will see how that strikes everybody. It will be a joy to people; everyone already rejoices that hostilities are about to commence. So insipid has life become for them. But you will see now, Sinclair, that is only the beginning. This will perhaps be a great war, a very great war. The new dispensation commences and for those who adhere to the old, the new will be terrible. What will you do?"

I was perplexed, everything sounded so strange and improbable.

"I don't know—and you?"

He shrugged his shoulders.

"As soon as mobilization orders are out, I join up. I am a lieutenant."

"You? I had no idea of that."

"Yes. It was one of my adaptations. You know, I have never wanted to appear out of the ordinary, and have rather done too much, in order to be correct, to do the right thing. In eight days, I think, I shall be already in the field."

"For God's sake!"

"Look here, old fellow, you mustn't take things so sentimentally. At bottom it certainly won't give me pleasure to order machine gunfire to be turned on living creatures, but that is a secondary matter. Now each one of us will be seized by the great wheel of fate. You as well. You will certainly be called up."

"And your mother, Demian?"

Then for the first time I recollected what I was doing a quarter of an hour before. How the world had changed! I had summoned together all my force in order to conjure up the sweetest picture, and now fate had suddenly put on a new, horrible mask.

"My mother? We need have no cares for her safety. She is safe, safer than anyone else in the world today. You love her so very much?"

"You knew it, Demian?" He laughed brightly and without any embarrassment.

"You child! Naturally I knew it. No one has yet called my mother Mother Eve without loving her. By the way, how was that? You have called to either her or myself today, haven't you?"

"Yes, I called—I called to Mother Eve."

"She felt it. She suddenly sent me away, I was to come to you. I had just told her the news about Russia."

We turned back, scarcely speaking, he untied his horse and mounted.

I first realized in my room how exhausted I was by Demian's message, and even more so by my previous spiritual exertions. But Mother Eve had heard me! My thoughts had reached her. She would have come herself, if—how wonderful all this was, and how beautiful! Now it was to be war. Now what we had so often spoken of was about to happen. And Demian had known so much in advance. How strange that the world's stream would no longer flow somewhere or other by us—that now it was suddenly flowing through us, that fate and adventure called us, and that now, or soon, the moment would come when the world would need us, when it would be transformed. Demian was right, one should not be sentimental over it. Only it was strange that I was now to experience that lonely thing, "fate," with so many, with the whole world. Good then!

I was ready. In the evening, when I went through the town, every corner was alive with bustle and excitement. Everywhere the word "war"!

I went to Mother Eve's house. We had supper in the summerhouse. I was the only guest. No one spoke a word about the war. But later, shortly before I left, Mother Eve said: "Dear Sinclair, you called me today. You know why I did not come myself. But don't forget, you know the call now and if ever you need someone who bears the sign, call me again."

She rose and went out through the gloaming into the garden. Tall and queenly, invested with mystery, she stepped between the trees, the foliage ceased its whispering at her approach, and over her head glimmered tenderly the many stars.

I am coming to the end. Events marched quickly. War was declared. Demian, who looked strange in uniform, with a silver-gray cloak, went away. I brought his mother home. Soon after I also said good-by to her. She kissed me on the lips and held me a moment on her breast, and her large eyes burned steadily close to mine.

And all men were like brothers. They had in mind their country and their honor. But it was fate, they peeped for a moment into the unveiled face. Young men came out of barracks, stepped into trains, and on many a face I saw a sign—not ours—a beautiful and dignified sign, signifying love and death. I as well was embraced by people I had never seen before. I understood and responded gladly. It was an atmosphere of intoxication in which they moved, not that of a fated will. But the intoxication was sacred, it was due to the fact that they had all looked into the rousing eyes of destiny.

It was already nearly winter when I went to the front.

At first, in spite of the sensation of the bombardment, I was disappointed with everything. Formerly I had often wondered why people so seldom were able to live for an ideal. Now I saw that many, yes, all men, are capable of dying for an ideal, provided that such an ideal is not personal, not chosen of their own free will. For them it had to be an ideal accepted by and common to a great number.

But with time I saw that I had underestimated men. Although service and a common danger renders them uniform, I saw many, living and dying, approach fate magnificently. Not only in an attack, but the whole time, many, very many of them had a fixed, far-away look, rather like that of a person possessed, a look which indicates entire ignorance of the end pursued, and a complete surrender of self to the unknown. No matter what they might believe and think they were ready, they were there in case of need, out of them would the future be formed. And, however strongly the world's attention appeared to be focused on war and heroic deeds, on honor and other old ideals, however distantly and unnaturally sang the voices of humanity—all this was merely the surface, just as the question with regard to the foreign and political aims of the war was superficial. Deep down, below the surface of human affairs, something was in process of forming. Something which might be a new order of humanity. For I could see many—many such died at my side—to whom the understanding was brought home that hate and rage, murder and destruction had no connection with the real object of the war. No, the object, just as the aims in view, was purely a matter of chance. Their deepest and most primitive feelings, even their wildest instincts were not actually directed against the enemy, their murderous and bloody work was an expression of their own inner being, of their cleft soul, which wished to rave and kill, to destroy and die, in order to be able to be born anew. A giant bird was fighting its way out of the egg, and the egg was the world, and the world had to go to ruin.

One night in early spring I was doing sentry duty in front of a farm we had occupied. The wind was blowing in fitful gusts, shrieking and moaning according to the vagaries of its mood; over the high Flanders sky rode an army of clouds, somewhere or other behind was a suspicion of moon. I had been restless throughout the whole of that day, troubled by cares which I could not precisely define. Now, at my dark post, I thought with fervor of the picture of my life up to that time, of Mother Eve, of Demian. I stood leaning against a poplar, staring into the agitated sky, the mysterious quivering brightness of which soon resolved itself into a series of pictures. I felt by the odd slowness of my pulse, by the insensibility of my skin to wind and rain, by the lively wakefulness of my inner being, that a guide was near me.

In the clouds a large city could be seen, out of which millions of men were streaming, spreading in swarms over the broad countryside. In their very midst there appeared the mighty figure of a god, as big as a mountain, with glittering stars in its hair, and with the features of

Mother Eve. Into it disappeared the processions of men, as into a gigantic cave, and were lost to view. The goddess shrank down on the ground, the sign on her forehead glittered brightly. She seemed to be under the influence of a dream. She closed her eyes and her large features were twisted in pain. Suddenly she cried out, and out of her forehead sprang stars, which hurried in lovely arcs and half-circles over the black sky.

One of the stars rushed noisily through the air to meet me, as if seeking me out. With a crash it burst into a thousand sparks, lifting me off my feet and hurling me on to the ground. The world broke up thunderously about me.

They found me close to the poplar, covered with earth and wounded in several places.

I lay in a cellar, guns growled and rumbled overhead. I lay in a cart, and was jolted over empty fields. For the most part I was either asleep or unconscious. But the more deeply I slept, the more strongly I felt that I was being drawn, that I followed at the will of a force over which I was not master.

I lay on straw in a stable, it was dark, someone trod on my hand. But my inner self willed to go further, the mysterious force drew me on. Again I lay in a cart, and later on a stretcher. Even more strongly I felt in me the command to go forward, I was conscious only of the pressure, the force which seemed to be controlling my journeying thus from place to place.

At last I was there. It was night. I was fully conscious and I felt strongly the secret attraction and power which had brought me to that place. Now I was lying in a room, on a bed made up on the floor. I felt I had arrived at the place to which I had been called. I glanced around, close to my mattress was another, on which someone was lying, someone who bent over and looked at me. It was Max Demian.

I could not speak, and he either could not or would not. He only looked at me. A lamp which hung over him on the wall cast a light on his face. He smiled at me.

For what seemed an immeasurably long time he gazed unwaveringly into my eyes. Slowly he inclined his face towards me, until we almost touched.

"Sinclair!" he said in a whisper.

I signaled to him with my eyes that I understood him. He smiled again, almost as if in compassion.

"Little one!" he said, smiling.

His mouth lay now quite close to mine. Softly he continued to speak.

"Can you still remember Frank Kromer?" he asked.

I winked at him, and could even manage to smile.

"Sinclair, old man, listen: I shall have to go away. Perhaps you will need me once again, on account of Kromer, or something. When you call me, I shall not come riding on a horse, or in a train. You must hearken to the voice inside you, then you will notice it is I, that

I am in you. Do you understand? And one other thing: Mother Eve said that if ever you were ill I was to give you a kiss from her, which she gave me. . . . Close your eyes, Sinclair!"

I obediently closed my eyes. I felt a light kiss on my lips, on which there was a trace of blood, which never seemed to stop flowing. And then I fell asleep.

In the morning I was awakened to have my wounds dressed. When at last I was properly awake, I turned quickly to the mattress by my side. A stranger lay upon it, a man on whom I had never before set eyes.

The bandaging hurt me. All that has happened to me since hurt me. But my soul is like a mysterious, locked house. And when I find the key and step right down into myself, to where the pictures painted by my destiny seem reflected on the dark mirror of my soul, then I need only stoop towards the black mirror and see my own picture, which now completely resembles Him, my guide and friend.

CPSIA information can be obtained
at www.ICGtesting.com
Printed in the USA
BVHW07045018122I
624328BV00003B/39